KU-239-443

HEARTSIDE BAY

Lovers and Losers

CATHY COLE

Scholastic Children's Books
An imprint of Scholastic Ltd
Euston House, 24 Eversholt Street, London, NW1 1DB, UK
Registered office: Westfield Road, Southam, Warwickshire, CV47 0RA
SCHOLASTIC and associated logos are trademarks and/or
registered trademarks of Scholastic Inc.

First published in the UK by Scholastic Ltd, 2014

Text copyright © Scholastic Ltd, 2014

ISBN 978 1407 14550 1

A CIP catalogue record for this book
is available from the British Library.

All rights reserved.
This book is sold subject to the condition that it shall not,
by way of trade or otherwise, be lent, hired out or otherwise circulated in
any form of binding or cover other than that in which it is published. No
part of this publication may be reproduced, stored in a retrieval system,
or transmitted in any form or by any means (electronic, mechanical,
photocopying, recording or otherwise) without prior
written permission of Scholastic Limited.

Printed by CPI Group (UK) Ltd, Croydon, CR0 4YY
Papers used by Scholastic Children's Books are made
from wood grown in sustainable forests.

1 3 5 7 9 10 8 6 4 2

This is a work of fiction. Names, characters, places, incidents
and dialogues are products of the author's imagination or are used
fictitiously. Any resemblance to actual people, living or dead,
events or locales is entirely coincidental.

www.scholastic.co.uk

FALKIRK COMMUNITY TRUST

30124 03005096 9

HEARTSIDE BAY

THE **HEARTSIDE BAY** SERIES

Cheers to
Lucy Courtenay and Sara Grant

Falkirk Council	
Askews & Holts	2015
JF T	£6.99

ONE

Rhi Wills sat up with a start as a wet, cold leaf landed on the end of her nose. The leaf fell soggily into her lap.

"That's a great look," teased Lila as Rhi picked up the leaf between her fingers and flicked it on to the grassy verge they were all sitting on.

"Very 'new age'," Eve drawled. "Perhaps we should all turn up to this festival wearing brown leaves."

"Stop being negative," scolded Eve's girlfriend Becca, flicking a lock of Eve's long auburn hair affectionately over her shoulder. "This festival may not have Prada on tap, but it's going to be really fun."

"If crazy hippies are your bag," said Eve, but she smiled at the same time.

Polly was lying with her head on her boyfriend Ollie's stomach. "I think brown leaves are sad," she said, sighing. "It means that summer's over."

Lila looked up from the comic she was working on with her boyfriend Josh just long enough to protest: "Not yet it isn't! We have a whole weekend left before school starts! And I don't know about you, but I plan to enjoy every moment."

Rhi could feel the dampness of the grass seeping through her jeans. Autumn was definitely in the air. She knew what Polly meant about being sad to see the back of summer. She'd had a fantastic couple of months, singing at gigs and festivals with her boyfriend Brody, feeling completely fulfilled in her music and earning more money than she had ever earned in her life. The Oak Horse Festival would be their last gig. She hoped it would be their best too.

Ollie checked his watch. "When is Brody going to show up with this van, then?" he asked.

Brody Baxter wasn't the best timekeeper in the world. Rhi knew that from having dated him for a few months. He was always late, but he was worth waiting for. "He'll show up when he shows up," she said with a shrug. "Think of it this way: at least it's a free ride."

"And at least it's not raining," Becca added.

"Yet," Eve said, in an ominous voice.

The Oak Horse Festival was deep in the woods, a couple of hours' drive from Heartside Bay. It was impossible to reach by public transport. Which was why Rhi and her friends were sprawled on a grassy verge on the edge of town, waiting for Brody and the van to show up.

Rhi thought about Brody's crystal blue eyes and warm smile. Their common love of music bound them together with golden threads, and she always felt contented and safe when she was with him. Brody always put her first. He made her feel like a better person. She hoped she had the same effect on him.

Max was so wrong for me, Rhi thought, picturing her ex-boyfriend's handsome face. Max Holmes could charm the birds from the trees, but underneath it all he had been a cheat. How had she put up with him for as long as she had? It was so strange to think of their relationship now. It was as if it had happened to a different person altogether.

As her friends continued moaning about the lateness of the van, Rhi felt a perfect sense of *belonging*. This weekend together at the Oak Horse Festival was going to be brilliant.

Suddenly, a battered grey van with rusty wheel arches rumbled around the corner. The most noticeable thing about it was the large spray-painted logo on the side, LOVERS AND LOSERS, scrawled in a riot of acid yellows and greens. With a squeal of brakes and the slight smell of burning rubber, the van screeched to a bumpy halt. Brody grinned at them out of the driver's window through his straw-blond fringe. He grinned extra wide at Rhi.

"Hop in then," he said.

"We're riding in *that*?" said Eve, looking appalled.

"Get *in*, your Royal Highness," Becca hissed, shoving Eve none too gently between the shoulder blades. "It's a free ride, remember?"

Everyone slung their bags into the back of the van, which smelled of diesel and damp. There were seats and windows, and plenty of space for their bags and camping equipment but that was about all that could be said of it.

"Next stop, hippy heaven," said Lila, giggling as Brody pulled away from the kerb in a gust of smelly diesel fumes.

"What kind of a band name is Lovers and Losers anyway?" Ollie asked over the rumble of the engine. "Who are the lovers and who are the losers?"

"They're all losers with a van like this," said Eve. "Ow, don't hit me, Becca."

"I'm a *loveur*," said Lila in an outrageous French accent, pursing her lips at Josh. "Are you a loveur too?"

"Loser all the way," said Josh amiably.

The next half an hour passed in a riot of jokes and challenges as everyone chose which camp they were in. Polly proclaimed that she was a loser, until Ollie shouted her down and kissed her dramatically to prove that she was in the lover camp.

"I'm definitely a lover," Eve announced. "I've dated boys *and* girls."

"And we all know how well the boy bit turned out," Becca remarked, to laughter from the others.

"Rhi's a lover," Brody shouted from the front of the van.

Rhi's friends whistled at her, and she blushed and

smiled. She *did* feel loved, no doubt about it. She wasn't going to argue.

The van clunked its way down the motorway. Ollie had brought snacks, which were swiftly eaten. They played memory games, and told stories, and speculated about what the new school year would bring. Following a toilet break at a service station, Brody swung the van off the motorway and into wilder, more wooded country. They started to see signs for the festival hanging from trees as they drove down roads that grew narrower with every passing mile. They finally turned down a rutted track marked with brightly coloured pennants, plunging beneath a canopy of trees still heavy with green foliage but browning a little at the edges.

The van bumped to a halt in a clearing full of tepees and several heavily decorated stages. There were some very strange people around, Rhi saw, as she helped the others unload the van. Barefooted children scampered past, their faces smeared with mud. There was a guy in a grubby white rabbit costume fixing mics on the stage, and a woman wearing a jumpsuit covered head to toe in rainbow feathers like it was the most normal thing in the world.

In the centre of the encampment stood the Oak Horse that Rhi guessed had given the festival its name. A giant structure of nailed wood and woven willow, with pennants for a mane and ribbons for a tail, the horse had a large wreath of leaves and flowers garlanding its neck. Children were climbing all over it, sitting astride it like bright-eyed monkeys. The sound of drumming filtered through the trees.

"Whoa," said Ollie with a snort of laughter. "How did you get this gig, guys? Communing with the tree spirits?"

There were stalls and food tents in the forest clearing with names like Faerie Aura, Moon Magic and the Chakra Café. Dreamcatchers hung in the trees, twisting and spinning and catching the light. There was a sign pointing to a sweat lodge somewhere deep in the trees. There were flyers for workshops called "Centring Your Chi" and "Reincarnation: The Truth", and the constant hum of a working wind turbine high above the tents. It wasn't the kind of festival Rhi had ever experienced before. It was a bit hippie, but she kind of liked it.

"Honoured guests! At last we meet!"

Rhi turned from the wind turbine to see two people with long tangled dark hair and a profusion of rainbow-coloured clothes bearing down on them with their arms extended. Lila stood grinning beside Rhi. Eve stayed behind Becca, while Ollie concentrated on holding Polly's hand and trying not to laugh. Polly looked genuinely happy to be here.

"Welcome!" repeated the woman. She was holding an armful of flower garlands, Rhi realized. "Let us cleanse you."

The cleansing seemed to consist of garlanding everyone's necks with the flowers and sprinkling them with something from an old leather pouch worn around the man's neck.

"Feels like they're seasoning us for dinner," Eve whispered as the glittering powder rained down on their heads.

"I think we're safe," Josh whispered back. "If there's such a thing as a vegetarian vibe, this place has it in spades."

"Hey, I love it here," Lila retorted, stroking the flowers around her neck. "It has a great vibe."

"Yeah, I like it too," said Polly. "What's wrong with

being vegetarian anyway?" she snapped, giving Josh a glare.

"Let the moon dust cleanse your auras and prepare your spirits for the Oak Horse," pronounced the man, still casting handfuls of powder into the air. "I'm Gerald by the way. And this is Kristina," he added, sounding more practical all of a sudden.

"You're the festival organizers, aren't you?" said Rhi in realization as the others exchanged baffled glances. "The ones who booked us to sing?"

Kristina smiled at Rhi. A gold tooth glittered inside her mouth. "This weekend with us will be a life-changing experience for you all," she said, looping the final garland around Becca's neck. "Let the Oak Horse into your hearts and rejoice!"

Rhi wasn't sure how to go about letting the Oak Horse into her heart. But she wasn't sure it mattered. She had the strangest feeling that Kristina was right – this weekend would be a life experience for all of them.

TWO

Becca had brought an enormous tent, big enough to fit everyone inside. Leaving Brody with Gerald and Kristina to sort out the details of his and Rhi's set the following day, the rest of them wandered into the woods in search of the perfect spot to pitch it. The woods were beautiful, Rhi thought, and very peaceful, if you could tune out the near-constant drumming from the festival site.

She was starting to feel a little guilty at bringing her friends to this place. The more people they saw wandering around the site in various states of undress, the more stalls and events and flags they registered, the clearer it became that these were hard-core hippies. Not really their style at all. This was a long way from their usual hangouts in Heartside Bay.

"I promise this is going to be fun, guys," she found herself saying as they walked on through the dappled light of the woodland.

Her friends smiled at her encouragingly.

"Don't worry, Rhi, we're not going to make a break for it," Josh promised.

"I love it here. And we have to hear you and Brody sing first, don't we?" Polly added. She sniffed the air. "That's a really good smell coming from the food tents. Falafels, I think. We should get some. And I smell chai-spiced tea."

"I keep thinking about what Josh said about the veggie vibe," Lila said, giggling. "He's right, you know. You could cause havoc in this place with a few rashers of bacon."

"Don't mention bacon," Ollie groaned.

Rhi felt a little better when Brody loped through the trees to join them. He was full of his usual positivity, which always brightened Rhi's own mood.

"Gerald and Kristina know what they're doing," Brody enthused. "They've been running this festival for twenty years, and they have all the gear. Our stage is great," he added, his eyes shining at Rhi. "It's in a tent with the most amazing striped interior you've ever seen. And guess what? The amps are powered by bicycles!"

"Bicycles?" echoed Josh. "You mean pedal power?"

"Yup," said Brody. "This place is so environmentally friendly, it's practically a tree."

Rhi loved the idea of seeing her friends pedalling away at the back of a tent to power the set. "You can take turns pedalling," she laughed. "We'll know if you're slacking."

Through the trees, she suddenly glimpsed a lone caravan, and a small piebald horse with its head in a headbag. The caravan was old, and built of wood in the traditional style, the outer slats painted green and the wheels black with rims picked out in red. It looked as if it had seen better days, with its peeling paint and battered, rusty-looking chimney through which a spiral of smoke was rising. A large sign decorated the caravan's side, stating in high old-fashioned lettering: MADAME FELICITY, TRUTH-TELLER.

"Very *Wizard of Oz*," said Eve, following Rhi's gaze.

Lila squealed. "Oh my god, a fortune teller! I've *always* wanted my fortune told!"

It did look like a fortune teller's caravan from a fairy story, now Rhi came to think of it. But not a very friendly one.

"Wow!" said Becca. "Count me in!"

"It could be fun, I suppose," said Eve thoughtfully.

Rhi wasn't sure she liked the gleam in her friends' eyes.

"It looks a bit creepy," said Polly, sounding as worried as Rhi felt.

"That's part of the fun!" Lila had already set off through the undergrowth towards the caravan.

"Count me out," said Ollie, shaking his head.

"I have better plans for this weekend than listening to a lot of mumbo-jumbo from a crazy old lady," Josh agreed.

Rhi watched as Becca and Eve chased after Lila, their laughter echoing through the trees. The horse stopped eating for a moment and whinnied softly.

"We can pitch camp if you guys want to join them," Brody offered. He drew Rhi into the warm circle of his arms and kissed her. "I don't need Madame Felicity," he said, smiling down at her. "I've seen our future already."

Rhi felt better. "There's probably no harm in it,"

she found herself saying to Polly. "Let's catch them up."

The caravan was even more moth-eaten close-up. Moss was growing on its patched roof, and an ancient iron kettle with a rusty spout was simmering on a scruffy little fire in front of the wooden steps. A clothes line had been strung between two trees, and faded garments flapped in the woodland air. The horse eyed them briefly, then went back to its nosebag.

"I don't like this," Polly said uncertainly.

Rhi could feel her nerve failing. She was about to suggest going back, when the caravan door burst open. Lila gave a little shriek. A figure with long, silvery hair appeared at the top of the steps, wearing a purple gown that seemed to float around her like water.

"Come inside, children. There is much to tell you."

Madame Felicity was beautiful, with heavily lidded violet eyes and silver rings on every finger. Her hair seemed to glow in the woodland air like a moonbeam. Her voice was deep and musical and oddly hypnotic.

Lila was the first one to climb the steps, entering the caravan at a sweeping gesture from Madame Felicity's arm.

"All of you," Madam Felicity said, as Rhi and the others hesitated on the grass. "All of you together. You have travelled together. You can learn together."

The caravan walls were swathed in midnight blue velvet, lit by groups of flickering candles. Sitting on the black draped table in the middle of the tiny wooden space was a large shining crystal ball.

I can't believe we're doing this, Rhi thought as everyone settled around the table, silent and awestruck. Polly's hazel eyes were almost as round as the crystal ball. Madame Felicity had a power that felt oddly irresistible.

"Now what?" inquired Eve, the first to break the silence.

Madame Felicity fixed Eve with her dark gaze. "Impatience with the world beyond brings nothing but disappointment," she said. "Wait and you will see."

Rhi found herself holding her breath as the fortune teller placed her long, slim hands on the ball. The twinkling lights around the walls made the silver rings on her fingers gleam.

"I see passion," she said. "I see fear. Ambition and love. I see it all."

Eve opened her mouth, most likely to say something sarcastic.

"I see many passionate relationships in your life," said the fortune teller, directing her gaze at Eve. "But first, there is something important that you must do. You, my dear, must find it in your heart to forgive your father even though he has done such wrong."

The colour drained from Eve's face. Becca took Eve's hand, looking alarmed. Rhi couldn't quite believe what the fortune teller had said. Eve had sworn she would never forgive her father for the fraud and bankruptcy he had inflicted on her family. But how would this fortune teller know that?

"I'll never forgive him," Eve whispered through stiff lips.

Madame Felicity nodded, as if she had expected Eve's answer. "Yes. But still, it must be done or your heart will be blocked for ever. You must forgive in order to set yourself free."

Her purplish eyes flicked over the crystal ball again, then moved to Polly, who was sitting beside Rhi. Polly gave an audible intake of breath.

"You have a rock in your life," said Madame

Felicity with approval. "This rock is your past, and your future."

Rhi thought, irrationally, of the rocks in the secret cove where she and her friends had spent so much time over the summer.

"This rock," Madame Felicity continued, "will keep you from drowning. You must trust the rock and trust yourself. That way you will be free from the worry in your mind."

Now it was Polly's turn to look shell-shocked. Rhi's brain started ricocheting around like a pinball. Drowning... Ollie had saved Polly from drowning only two weeks ago... *Ollie was the rock.* And Polly was the biggest worrier she knew. How could Madame Felicity have known that?

The dark blue velvet of the caravan's interior seemed to press closer around them. Rhi hardly dared to look at the fortune teller. Suddenly, she didn't want to hear about herself at all.

"What about me?" said Lila breathlessly, her eyes shining.

"The free spirit is strong in you, my dear." Madame Felicity's hands passed over the ball, weaving complicated patterns on its smooth, glassy surface. "You must not lose it, for it holds the key to your destiny."

Lila looked a little disappointed. It seemed she had been hoping for something clearer than that.

"Can you see anything for me?" Becca asked quietly.

The fortune teller smiled. Her hair seemed to glow even more brightly. "You must find your home, my dear," she said. "Or you will never find true love. Your path has been hard, but it grows easier with every step you take towards the truth."

Now it was Eve's turn to hold Becca's hand, as her girlfriend turned as pale as the fortune teller's silvery hair.

Don't look at me, Rhi prayed, although she knew that the fortune teller would. *Don't tell me anything. I don't want to know.*

The rational part of her knew that this was all wild guesses and fancy props. A crystal ball, glowing lights. Party tricks, all of them. And yet...

The fortune teller turned her eyes on Rhi. Rhi felt the oddest sensation, as if she had just plunged into an icy pool. Her skin prickled into goosebumps. She didn't seem able to deflect Madame Felicity's gaze. The fortune teller was looking inside her. Right into her soul. And was it her imagination, or was the crystal ball glowing brighter?

She heard the fortune teller's voice from somewhere far away.

"Your music will endure. Your partnership too. Your songs are from your hearts, and the spirits have heard. Great fame and fortune lie ahead. Hands raised in celebration before you, voices raised in song together. You and the boy..."

Rhi could hardly breathe. The fortune teller's eyes were so deep and strange.

"You and the boy," the fortune teller repeated. "Do not mistake what you have, my dear. Do not confuse the muse with love."

Tears blurred stupidly in Rhi's eyes as she realized what the fortune teller was saying.

She and Brody weren't meant to be together. The music that they made was pure magic, but the rest... The rest was an illusion.

THREE

It couldn't be true, Rhi thought numbly. She and Brody were right for each other. You only had to listen to them singing together to know that.

Isn't that the point? said the small, doubting voice in her head. *You and Brody are all about the music?*

Rhi didn't want to believe it, but the thought was there, nagging at her. She had never intended to date Brody in the first place, but somehow – it had happened. *What we have is great*, she told herself fiercely.

"I don't believe you," she said out loud.

"Believe what you wish, my dear. I only tell you the things that I see."

Rhi exchanged glances with the others. Everyone

was looking pale and shocked. Why had they come to this place? What were they doing, listening to this crazy old woman and her magic tricks?

Madame Felicity suddenly held up her hands. Her eyes seemed to glow a deeper shade of violet.

"There is more," she said, in a tone that made Rhi feel more nervous than ever.

The fortune teller placed her hands once more on the glowing crystal ball. Something was moving in the core of the crystal, swirling and twisting. Rhi shook her head, trying to clear the odd oppressive feeling, but she couldn't tear her eyes away. Shadow and light shifted. And, for the briefest instant, she glimpsed a boy's face, dark and sneering. Rhi had barely blinked when the image vanished, leaving only a faint memory dancing through her mind.

"Heed me well," said Madame Felicity, so quietly that they all strained across the table to hear her. "Beware the stranger in your midst. He brings dark discord."

This was getting seriously crazy.

"What stranger? Who is he? Have we met him yet?" Lila squeaked. Her voice sounded rusty, like she hadn't used it in a while.

"Call me a psychic, but I'm guessing not," said Eve in a barbed tone of voice. "The clue is in the word, Lila. 'Stranger'?"

"Shh," said Polly, looking alarmed and fiddling restlessly with the black cloth covering the table. "Don't be rude, Eve. Not here. It doesn't feel ... right."

Rhi knew what Polly meant. This caravan had a strange feel to it, like they weren't quite in the real world. Anywhere else Rhi would have laughed at Madame Felicity's formal and bizarre proclamations. But here in the caravan, it seemed all too believable.

Madame Felicity seemed to have taken offence. She stood up in a single flowing motion. "I have said enough," she said curtly. "Leave now."

She extended her arms so that her sleeves fell like lilac wings, filling the tiny velvet space and making it feel cramped and unwelcoming.

"I *told* you, you shouldn't have been rude, Eve," Polly whispered unhappily as Rhi and the others stood up from the table and shuffled out of the caravan, down the wooden steps and back to the rusty kettle, the crackling camp fire and the grumpy-looking horse.

The door closed firmly. The fortune teller had gone.

"Whoa," said Becca, the first to speak. "Was that weird or what?"

Rhi felt exhausted, her mind as wrung out as Madame Felicity's washing flapping on the clothes line. She didn't know what to think. Maybe she had misunderstood the fortune teller's words.

"Come on, you're not believing all that stuff, are you?" Eve scoffed, looking around at the pale faces of her friends as they walked a little unsteadily back through the trees towards where they had left the boys with the tent.

"It was weird," Becca repeated. Her freckled face was unusually serious, and her green eyes dark. "She *knew* things. You could say I haven't had a home for ten years now."

"It was all a show," Eve insisted. "Smoke and mirrors. Impressive, but completely untrue."

"But she knew about your father, Eve," Polly pointed out, a little cautiously. "She knew you haven't spoken to him in a while—" Eve's dad was in prison for fraud and Eve hadn't been in touch with him at all since his court case.

Eve's grey eyes flashed sharply. "She knows *nothing*."

"She was right about my free spirit," Lila said happily.

"Anyone looking at you could figure that out," Eve said, looking pointedly at Lila's floaty dress and the braids that she'd put in her long dark hair in anticipation of the festival.

Lila ignored that. "I wish she'd said something about Josh and me though. You're so lucky, Polly. You and Ollie are written in the crystal ball."

While Brody and I aren't, Rhi thought a little numbly. Could it be true, what the fortune teller had said? She didn't know what to think.

"It was spooky, wasn't it, the bit about my rock?" Polly said shyly. She'd hennaed her hair especially for the weekend, and it caught the sunlight filtering through the trees over their heads. "Ollie *is* my rock. I'm sure we'll be together for ever, like she says. But it was creepy, the way she knew about the drowning thing. There was definitely something strange about her."

Becca and Lila made noisy sounds of agreement.

"She knew nothing," Eve repeated stubbornly.

Lila turned her dark blue eyes on Eve. "She's right. About your dad, I mean. You do need to forgive him, Eve."

Eve shook her head, like she had water in her ears, clearly keen to change the subject. "What about Rhi?" she said, glancing in Rhi's direction. "We haven't talked about Madame Weirdo's prediction for the musical superstar in our midst yet. Even *I* could have worked that one out. I mean, look at her! Fame and fortune in the making!"

Rhi felt a little better as her friends all grinned at her.

"And she was wrong about Brody," Eve pointed out with some satisfaction. "Rhi and Brody are a perfect pair, romantically *and* musically."

Rhi would have agreed with Eve barely half an hour earlier. Now, she only hoped it was true.

"I hope our gig tomorrow goes OK," she said out loud.

"Your gig is going to rock these woodland spirits out of the trees," Lila pronounced, linking arms with Rhi.

"As long as we all keep pedalling," Becca laughed.

"Do you think we should tell the boys what she said?" Polly asked. She looked a little anxious at the thought.

"No," said Eve at once. "We should keep it to ourselves. Agreed?"

It was always hard to argue with Eve. Lila agreed a little sulkily. Becca shrugged. Polly simply looked relieved. The boys were bound to scoff, Rhi knew.

"Come on," said Eve, speeding up. "I don't want to waste another second thinking about Miss Spooky Shoes and her little wooden house on wheels. This is a festival. I plan to enjoy myself in the mud and the mayhem. Somehow."

Despite her unwillingness to believe anything Madame Felicity had said, questions were crowding Rhi's mind. If she didn't ask them now, perhaps she wouldn't get another chance.

"Do you ever wonder if your future is already determined?" she asked the others as they reached the campsite. "Or do you think we truly control our own destinies?"

"We control our own lives, end of story," said Eve. "How can it be otherwise? We're the ones who make the decisions. Our brains, our choices."

"I think it's probably a bit of both," said Polly. She swiped at the undergrowth where it was trying to catch at the dress she was wearing. "We're specks in the universe, if you think about it. It's arrogant to think that we know *everything* about how the universe works."

"It's a bit like horoscopes, isn't it?" Lila asked. "There are definite characteristics that people share when they're a Leo, for example, or Scorpio. And that's out of our control, isn't it?"

Eve made her arm into the curling tail of a scorpion and swooped down to 'sting' Lila in the neck. When Lila had stopped squealing, the conversation turned to creepy-crawlies in the woods, and sharing stories of wasps and mosquitoes and other flying things. Rhi, on the other hand, found herself still brooding about Madame Felicity's vision of her life, and the dangerous stranger due to come into their lives.

It doesn't have to be that way, she thought. *I can change Madame Felicity's predictions about my future. What does she know? She's a crazy lady in a caravan. Brody and I are meant to be, and that's the end of that.*

FOUR

The boys almost had the tent up when the girls arrived at the site. The large canvas structure flapped a little unevenly in the breeze, but it was upright and the pegs had been driven firmly into the ground. Brody had even rigged a little pennant at the top of the tent, which fluttered in jaunty shades of yellow and orange.

"Wow!" Lila exclaimed as they stopped, all feeling a little breathless from their walk through the woods, and admired the result of the boys' hard work. "This is fantastic!"

"You could fit a family of bears in here," Becca remarked, peering through the tent flaps to the great space inside, arranged around a central pole.

"It's going to smell like a family of bears live here

too," Eve said. "Can we have a rule that all socks have to be packed away the moment you take them off, boys?"

"Ollie and Brody did most of it," said Josh, looking up from where he was comfortably sprawled among the roots of a large oak tree nearby, his sketch pad in his hand.

"All of it," Ollie corrected, wiping his forehead with his forearm and smiling warmly down at Polly as she snuggled into his arms for a kiss.

"Fair comment," Josh said with a shrug. "I'm paying my way with pictures."

Lila draped her arms around Josh's neck and peered down at his sketch pad. "These are brilliant," she giggled. "I love the look on Ollie's face in that one."

"That'll be when he dropped the hammer on his toe," Josh replied, grinning. He tipped his hat back from his face as Lila planted a kiss on his cheek.

All Rhi wanted was to see Brody. She desperately needed reassurance. For all her good intentions not to listen to a word the fortune teller had said, she could feel the doubt squirming in her belly. She needed to see him. If she could kiss him and talk to him, she would know that everything was going to be OK.

"Hey," said Brody, emerging from the tent. "Did you guys have fun?"

Rhi leaped into his arms, taking him by surprise, and kissed him hard. Brody responded at once, lifting her off the ground and kissing her back even harder. The tingles now whooshing through her belly firmly dispatched the wormy doubts. They felt so good together. This was right. The thrill of him, his lips and his arms, was as perfect as ever. Madame Felicity could keep her gloomy predictions. She hadn't seen a grim-faced stranger in the ball at all. No one and nothing could stop her from being with Brody if she wanted to be.

"What was that for?" said Brody, sounding a little dazed as Rhi broke the kiss first.

"You," Rhi said, dabbing her finger on the end of his nose. "Because you're gorgeous and I'm crazy about you." She *was*. She *was* crazy about him.

"Don't mention the word crazy," said Ollie, now sitting comfortably on a rug that Eve had pulled out of her bag. "There are way too many crazies running around this place for comfort. I heard two guys talking about dragons about fifteen minutes ago. Seriously. Dragons."

Lila giggled, snuggled in Josh's lap among the tree roots. "Josh has drawn one of them in his sketchbook. There's smoke coming out of the guy's nose, look."

"There is so much fantastic material here," Josh said as everyone marvelled at his witty drawing. "I'm not into this new age stuff, but it's really great to draw."

"Ow," said Brody.

Rhi realized she had been squeezing his hand very hard. She let go a little sheepishly. "Sorry," she said.

He gently brushed her cloud of dark curls out of her eyes. "What's up, Rhi? You seem jumpy."

"I'm not jumpy," said Rhi. Was she jumpy? She didn't think she was jumpy. "I'm fine." She tried to hold his crystal clear gaze, but found her eyes darting sideways.

"Are you nervous about the gig?"

Maybe it *was* the gig, Rhi thought. This festival was unlike any other event they'd performed at. Bicycle-powered amps, for starters. For a brief moment, she wondered whether to tell Brody about Madame Felicity's prediction, about the stranger she had glimpsed in the ball, but she crushed the thought immediately.

31

"Yes," she said aloud. "I think I am."

He slipped his arm around her waist. "You need a little music. I'll show you our stage, and then we can go and play somewhere together. Sound good?"

He picked up his guitar from where it stood propped up against the tent, took Rhi by the hand, and led her through the woods and out into the thick of the festival. They wove among stalls selling incense and fairy wings, drums and yoga mats and kites in the form of dragons, until they came to a large brown tent bearing their names outside on a chalkboard.

It was cool and dark inside. The promised bicycles were at the back of the tent, wired up to a generator. It was currently being pedalled by a large lady in tie-dyed harem pants who looked like she was enjoying the exercise. Someone was on the stage with a long-necked sitar in his lap, and the soothing music bounced around the canvas walls as they watched.

"We'll get the others to take turns on the bike when we're playing," Brody said, as they came outside again. "This is going to be legendary. Let's go explore."

They walked hand in hand past campfires, dancers moving among the trees, and stalls selling crystals, clothing and jewellery. Until at last they left the crowds behind and the woodland grew still and peaceful.

They reached a gently bubbling brook and jumped over stones and twigs on the forest floor. Brody unslung his guitar and sat on an upturned tree trunk. Rhi sat on the bank, and enjoyed the cool feel of the water on her feet.

"I've written a new song," Brody said. His eyes were clear and serious, and full of affection. "It's for you."

Rhi's heart jumped. She loved it when Brody wrote new songs. She lay back on the mossy ground, water still running briskly over her feet, and listened as he played, feeling the sun dappling on her closed eyelids. The music was just like the brook, she realized, strong and true and lively, and she bobbed her toes in the water to the beat of the quick strumming strings.

"Beautiful," she breathed as Brody finished the lilting tune with a touch of high, pure harmonics at the tops of his strings.

He set his guitar down in the moss beside her, and leaned gently over her to press his lips to hers.

"And so are you," he whispered.

He did complete her, Rhi thought, awash with pleasure as she twisted her arms around his neck to kiss him more deeply. Madame Felicity knew nothing. She was a sideshow, smoke and mirrors. It was just like Eve said. How could she have doubted it for an instant?

"Sing it again," she begged, sitting up after a few minutes.

Brody picked a few leaves out of her hair and took up his guitar again. "The music in you and the music in me," he sang, smiling across the fretboard at her, "they tie us together while making us free, they tie us together while making us free."

Strings, lilting harmonics. The brook flashed along, chattering quietly. It was perfect. And suddenly Rhi felt a stone settling in her belly as she listened.

"The song is the magic, the tune is the spell, and we are magicians to weave them so well, and we are magicians to weave them so well..."

Music, she thought. *It's just like Madame Felicity said. It's all about the music. Nothing more than that.*

"The rhythms are dancing, the harmonies too, the music in me and the music in you," Brody sang, bringing the song to its conclusion, "the music in me ... and the music in you."

The chord echoed away off the trees and faded into the bubbling sounds of the brook.

"Sums us up," Brody said, leaning down to kiss Rhi again. "Don't you think?"

And Rhi's heart broke clean in two because he was right.

FIVE

Rhi didn't have the heart to make much in the way of conversation with Brody for the rest of the afternoon. They walked around the festival site hand in hand, looking at crystals and henna hand-painting, and watching stilt walkers in tall red hats moving among the trees like alien beings. Brody seemed to accept that she was nervous about the following night's gig. He kissed her a lot, and held her, and did his best to cheer her up.

"Last gig of the summer, Rhi," he promised as they made their way back to their campsite in the dimming light of the evening. "And we're going to smash it. We'll be taking bookings for next summer before you know it."

They walked past the Oak Horse with its flowing ribbon tail, put Brody's guitar safely in the van and then wended their way through a copse of closely packed birch trees to where a campfire was glowing brightly outside their tent.

The others had been hard at work decorating the tent while Rhi and Brody were out. Now the whole space, inside and out, was full of rugs and cushions, and candles hung in jam jars from the tree branches over their heads. It looked magical.

"The lovers return!" Ollie exclaimed, raising a large bottle of lemonade at Brody and Rhi as they moved into the fire-lit circle. "We decided the tree spirits had got you."

"Have you noticed how mobile reception is really bad out here?" Eve said, examining her phone by the light of the fire.

"Who needs a mobile when you can commune with your soul?" Josh enquired, to much giggling.

There was a pot simmering on the campfire, Rhi realized. "What have you been making?" she asked, peering into its warm, scented depths.

"Baked beans with extra veggies," announced Becca.

"And salami," Ollie added, waving a fat salami sausage in the air. "I packed one just in case."

"The tent tonight is going to smell terrible," said Lila, and everyone groaned at the prospect.

Rhi sprawled on the cushions with a bowl of beans and a bread roll, and listened to her friends talking and laughing together in the firelight. Somewhere among the trees, the drummers were still beating their endless dreamy rhythms, and the repetitive sound felt like the heartbeat of the festival.

After dinner, Brody got out his guitar and took requests. They almost blew the campfire out with their loud rendition of "Fast Lane Freak". They were left very much alone in their little wooded island of privacy among the trees. Everything about the evening was perfect, and Rhi's fears about her and Brody seemed to lessen as the sun slowly set.

All summers should be like this, she thought dreamily as the boys roasted bananas and chocolate wrapped in foil over the campfire. *I could stay like this for ever and ever.*

Over several bags of popcorn, the boys started coaxing some facts about Madame Felicity out of the girls.

"You have to tell us something," Josh wheedled, his arm wrapped loosely around Lila's shoulders. "Was she a hag with a snaggle-tooth? Did she have a one-eyed cat? Give me details, people. I want to draw her."

"She was beautiful," said Polly, in a faraway voice. "Magical. Like moonlight."

"It was her hair," Rhi supplied, thinking back to the strange silver-haired woman. With food and coffee in her belly, the whole experience felt like an odd moment from the distant past. "It shone like a moonbeam."

"Did she mention any tall, dark, handsome strangers?" Brody inquired, raising his eyebrows.

"Why are tall handsome strangers always dark?" objected Ollie, and Polly rubbed his blond hair in consolation.

"She did say something about a stranger, now you come to mention it," said Eve.

Rhi stiffened. She didn't want to think about the face she'd seen in the crystal ball.

"Is he going to sweep someone off their feet?" Josh asked. "It had better not be Lila. She's taken." He kissed his girlfriend lingeringly.

"It was creepier than that," Becca said. "'Dark discord' were the words she used."

"Ooh," said Ollie, and made a spooky face.

"Dark discord is a great name for a song," said Brody. "Don't you think, Rhi?"

Everyone started speculating on what dark discord this stranger was likely to cause. Would he appear at the festival? Or back in Heartside Bay when they least expected it? *He's not real!* Rhi wanted to shout. The memory of the boy's face in the crystal ball teased her. *How do you know I'm not real?* he seemed to say, with a dark smile.

"I have a bad feeling about him," said Polly.

"You have bad feelings about everyone," said Ollie as he kissed the top of her head.

"I'm worried he'll split us all up."

It was only when everyone looked at her that Rhi realized she'd spoken. She flushed. She hadn't meant to say that out loud.

"Never!" Eve brandished her coffee cup like a weapon. "We are one. Nothing will ever come between us."

"I'll drink to that," said Ollie, raising his lemonade again.

40

The campfire was dying down now, and most of the candles in the jam jars had guttered out. Somewhere in the trees behind them, a woodland creature screeched, making everyone jump. A barn owl, perhaps, or a fox. Moonlight filtered through the leaves and striped the air with pale light. Maybe it wasn't moonlight, Rhi thought irrationally. Maybe it was Madame Felicity flitting among the trees, her hair streaming down her back.

Rhi didn't feel tired. She felt unnerved and edgy. She felt like she was being watched. The woods around her were alive with sounds: rustling, squeaking, echoing.

"What's that?" said Eve suddenly.

The moonlight in their little glade seemed to intensify. The campsite was encircled, Rhi realized with a stab of horror. Columns of light were all around...

She screamed. The others leaped out of their skins. Suddenly, all was confusion.

"Hey!" said Brody, catching Rhi around the waist. "It's OK—"

Rhi screamed again, and struck at Brody with her fists. Couldn't he feel it? A deep and primal instinct was roaring through her, telling her to get away from this place and its shadows—

"Excuse me," said a polite voice. "Are we in the right place for the moon festival?"

A group of people – men and women dressed in long white silky-looking robes – were standing around their tent, looking enquiringly at them. Rhi's sense of terror resolved itself into embarrassment. She had thought... What had she thought, exactly? That these were ghosts? The spirit of Madame Felicity out to haunt her? It all seemed so stupid now.

"No moon festivals here," said Becca. "Sorry."

The man who had spoken looked disappointed. Rhi saw that he had a crescent moon painted in white on his forehead.

"We must have taken a wrong turn at the Aura Dome, Kevin," said a very ordinary-looking woman with long blonde hair.

A few members of the group were raising their hands to the moonlight and swaying gently on the spot. Rhi could see that Ollie was struggling not to laugh. Lila had lost the battle already, and was giggling hopelessly into her hands. This was all so *bizarre*.

"I can escort you back to the main site, if you like?"

offered Josh. "I'm sure you can find someone to ask there."

"That would be kind," Kevin beamed. "You are all very welcome to join our ritual, if you would like to? We bathe our naked bodies in the moonlight and welcome the healing powers of the moon goddess. It's most refreshing."

"That sounds very interesting," said Polly politely as Ollie lost his battle and dissolved into silent helpless laughter beside Lila. "But I'm afraid we're going to bed soon."

"I'll walk with Josh," Brody told Rhi, as Josh started trying to usher the white figures through the trees like sheep in a field. "Are you going to be OK?"

"Fine," Rhi mumbled. "Sorry I screamed like that."

Brody's teeth gleamed in the moonlight. "This place is full of surprises. What's one more?"

As he jogged gently after Josh, the blonde woman's voice floated towards them through the trees.

"We should have turned *left* at the Aura Dome, Kevin. I did tell you..."

Rhi felt a giggle rising in her throat. She clapped her hands to her mouth as the laughter came pouring out of her. Eve and Becca started holding each other, laughing so hard they looked like they were about to fall over. Ollie and Lila were beyond that stage already.

"Ow," Lila moaned, clutching at her belly. "I can't laugh any more. Please, my stomach is going to split!"

It had been a *very* strange day.

SIX

They laughed for a good half hour after the moon bathers had left.

"Honestly," said Eve, wiping her eyes as Becca threw another log on the campfire, making the embers crackle and leap back into life. "Who *were* those people?"

"Well, one of them was called Kevin," said Ollie seriously, which set them off again.

"It must be nice to come to a festival like this if you're a hippy," said Polly. "Unlike in real life, you can do all these crazy things and no one turns a hair."

"Imagine if they tried naked moon dancing on the beach at Heartside," Rhi laughed.

Ollie looked thoughtful. "I like that idea."

A crackling of twigs underfoot made them all look up from the fire. Brody and Josh had made it back to the campsite in one piece.

"I bet you joined in," Lila teased, kissing Josh.

"Did they really take their clothes off?" Eve asked, sounding a little disapproving.

"Kevin did," said Brody. He settled down beside Rhi, hugging her close. "But most of the others kept their gowns on."

Josh's eyes were gleaming in the firelight. "My fingers are itching to get it all down on paper. They formed this circle around a woodland pond reflecting the moon and just went crazy." He flapped his arms around to demonstrate, and almost knocked his own hat off.

"Wasn't it spooky?" Polly wanted to know.

"I suppose it was, a little," said Brody. "If you half closed your eyes, the people kind of disappeared. All you could see were their white gowns floating around by themselves."

"Headless ghosts," Ollie intoned. "Indulging in the dance of *death*."

There was a delighted intake of breath around the fire. Encouraged by this response, Ollie lowered his voice. "They were sacrificed to the moon goddess a thousand years ago. Their heads torn from their bodies and their hearts cast into the woodland pond. Now they rise again once a year in a desperate bid to return to life."

Eve shivered agreeably. "No wonder they invited us to join them. Fresh meat, warm blood . . . all the things they have lost. . ."

Polly squeaked and snuggled closer to Ollie. Rhi felt a prickle of the unease she'd experienced earlier in the evening. The way the moon dancers had converged on the campsite, their white gowns whispering on the forest floor. . . It was no great leap of imagination to change them into ravaged headless zombies. . . She snuggled in to Brody a little more closely.

"This area is famous for its witches," said Becca. "Shall I tell you the terrible tale of Skinless Meg?"

Rhi's unease doubled. She had always hated scary stories.

"Sounds awesome," said Ollie in excitement. "How did she lose her skin?"

Becca stood up. Her fire-lit shadow stretched away from her into the woods.

"There once was a witch who ate the toes of children. She would steal into the village at night with a blade of iron and slice away her dinner. Slice, slice!"

Ollie and Josh laughed in uneasy appreciation. Becca smiled ghoulishly. "Meg roasted them on her witch's fire and gnawed the sweet morsels of flesh and made a necklace with the bones. The villagers came for Meg one night, armed with blades of their own. They caught her and tied her to a tree and took a long strip of flesh from her body for every toe that she'd stolen. Soon there was nothing left of Meg but blood and bone."

"That is so gross," Lila squealed, hiding her head in her hands.

Becca went on relentlessly: "She haunts these woods today, her iron blade glinting. Looking for skin to replace her own. Her toe-bone necklace clatters when she approaches, but no one ever hears the blade as it whistles towards them. Slice. Slice. *Slice*..."

On the last word, Becca lunged towards Eve with her fingers curled into claws. Eve let out a genuine scream, to the instant amusement of the boys.

"I'm zipping my sleeping bag all the way to the top tonight," said Polly with a shiver.

Ollie told a ghost story about a pirate next, but the story washed over Rhi. She found herself straining for the sound of Meg's clattering toe-bone necklace in the dark night. Her skin was prickling. Madame Felicity and her predictions were back on her mind.

She felt Brody stroking the back of her neck with his fingers. She looked up at him and smiled. Brody was here. She was safe.

"Boo," he whispered.

Rhi gave herself up to his kiss, losing herself in the rightness of her feelings. Ghosts and ghouls and skinless witches faded away. With Brody's lips on hers, anything was possible. Madame Felicity was wrong.

Breaking away from Brody, Rhi realized that the ghost stories had petered out. Eve and Becca were curled up in the shadows. Lila and Josh were whispering to each other and giggling. With her head resting on Ollie's shoulder, Polly smiled sleepily across the guttering campfire at Rhi.

"I'm almost ready to head to bed," Ollie said with a yawn.

Lila turned towards them. "Not yet," she begged.

"This evening has been too nice to end. Brody, Rhi – can't you sing another song or something?"

"My guitar's in the van," said Brody. "I'll go and fetch it, as long as you all promise not to be asleep by the time I get back."

Rhi's bladder was complaining. She'd been putting off the moment for as long as she could, but she couldn't wait any longer. Where were the festival toilets anyway? She and Brody had passed them earlier, in a private stretch of woodland some way from their campsite. She had a nasty feeling they were back over on the far side of the festival, miles from the tent.

Rhi wasn't sure she wanted to go on her own, but everyone else had settled back down to chatting and snuggling with their partners. She didn't particularly want to interrupt. And so, suppressing a sigh at the prospect of the long walk, Rhi headed towards the festival site, counting campfires as she went in a bid not to get lost.

Everything looked different in the dark. She stopped uncertainly by the Oak Horse and scanned the site. Tents glowed in many and various colours around her, their fires dying down for the night. The Oak

Horse watched her with dark eyes as she passed, and she wrapped her arms around herself to ward off the sudden chill. She recognized a path she and Brody had taken earlier and headed down it, sighing with relief as she turned a bend and saw the toilets ahead.

Her mission to the toilet block a success, Rhi decided to walk back to the campsite through the woods. There were fewer tents to fall over and guy ropes to negotiate.

The trees muffled the sounds of the festival as soon as she left the path. Keeping her eyes firmly on where she judged the campsite to be, Rhi moved among the trunks, taking care not to trip on the tree roots.

As she moved further from the lights of the festival, the moon dipped behind a cloud and the forest was cloaked in sudden darkness. Rhi stopped. She could still pick out the campfires once her eyes had adjusted, and so she moved onwards again after a moment, a little more slowly this time. Nameless fears stirred in her gut, fluttering on silent wings.

There's nothing to be scared of, Rhi told herself.

The darkness felt as if it was growing. The campfires she had been keeping in her sights vanished behind trunks, branches and leaves. Rhi found herself longing for a burst of moonlight to still her jumpy heart.

There was a rustling in the trees behind her. A freakishly large badger's head loomed before her like a horrible striped mirage. Rhi's heart crashed in her chest from shock, and she cried out in fright, pressing herself against the nearest tree.

"Beasts of the night!" cried the mask.

A fox slid into view, then an owl with long ragged tree-bark wings and whirlpool eyes.

"Beasts of the night, hunters of the woods!" shrieked the owl, to shouts of wild laughter from the fox.

The owl seemed to swoop at Rhi. More figures appeared, wearing great lumpen animal heads that sat unevenly on their shoulders, yelling and calling. Rhi was unable to shake the paralysing terror that beneath the masks lurked the flayed face of Skinless Meg, her toe-bones clattering...

"Rhi! RHI! Where are you, Rhi?"

Brody was calling her. She had to find him. She stumbled on. *I'm here! Help me...*

A figure slid into focus in a shadowy clearing,

a flash of blond hair, arms reaching out. Rhi ran into Brody's arms, and pulled him towards her for a passionate kiss. Flames flickered through her as the kiss deepened, easing her fear, and the only thing that mattered was this—

And then somehow it was Ollie standing with his arms around her, his eyes wide and blue and startled. Rhi gazed at him in disbelief. They had just... She and Ollie had...

She had just kissed entirely the wrong person.

SEVEN

Rhi wrenched herself from Ollie's arms as if she had been electrocuted. How had this happened? How could she have made such a mistake? It had been Brody calling her, she had felt sure of it... But the shadows, the darkness, her dreadful fear... Somehow it had all conspired to bring her to this.

She stumbled backwards, her cheeks flaming, willing the whole scene to be a dream. Her lips still burned from Ollie's kiss. *They had kissed for real.* Her heel caught in a tree root and brought her down to the uneven forest floor with a bump.

To Rhi's absolute horror, Brody now appeared at Ollie's shoulder. "What's going on?" her boyfriend asked.

"I..." Rhi stammered. How could she explain this

without sounding completely crazy?

Ollie rubbed his chin. "Don't look at me, mate. Rhi jumped on me from nowhere."

"You did *what*, Rhi?"

How long had Polly been standing there? Rhi's brain skittered around her head like a mouse in a trap as she saw how Polly had pressed her hands to her cheeks, her mouth open in a perfect O of shock.

"Babe," said Ollie, flushing bright red before the wide stare of his girlfriend, "I know this looks bad, but seriously, it was nothing to do with me!"

Everyone looked at each other in the stretching silence. *What have I done?* Rhi thought in anguish.

Polly made a choking noise. "How could you?" she screamed at Rhi, before blundering away into the darkness.

Ollie seemed to come to his senses. He spun around helplessly, trying to see where Polly had gone. "Poll!" he bawled, giving chase. "It's not what it looked like... I swear I don't know what happened..."

Rhi wanted to die of humiliation. She could hardly bear to think what Polly – dear, loving, fragile Polly – was thinking right now. *That must have looked bad,* she thought dimly. *Really, really bad*. This place was really messing with her head...

"Are you planning on standing up any time soon?" Brody asked.

Rhi tried to get up, but her legs wouldn't obey her. Brody held out his hands, and she took them, cringing with embarrassment. He was looking quizzically at her, and she could hardly meet his gaze.

"Did you seriously just kiss Ollie?" He sounded genuinely curious.

"I ... owl..." she blurted. Nothing sensible was coming out of her mouth. It all seemed so stupid now she was with Brody. He and Ollie looked nothing like each other at all. Brody was much slighter, his hair longer. No one would believe that she'd muddled the two boys up. She hardly believed it herself.

"Take your time," said Brody, looking increasingly mystified.

"I met these people all dressed up in the woods. They were wearing masks: an owl, a badger... They spooked me and I just ran back to the campsite. I wasn't thinking straight. I saw you, only it wasn't you. Brody, I made a stupid mistake. I thought..." Rhi gazed helplessly in the direction of Ollie's muffled yells and Polly's dimming sobs. "I thought Ollie was you."

Brody snorted. "I don't often get mistaken for school football stars. I guess I should be flattered. Was he a good kisser?"

Rhi saw a flash of pain in his eyes as he tried to sound casual about the question, and she felt miserable for causing it. She remembered the flick of fire she had felt at the touch of Ollie's lips against hers. "I have no idea," she said, trying to sound casual. "We didn't get too far before I realized my mistake."

That wasn't exactly true, Rhi knew, and she squirmed at the lie. It was awkward to admit that there had been a moment when Ollie's lips had locked on to hers and... It hadn't meant anything, of course, but still... The kiss had felt way too good for comfort.

"I'm so embarrassed," she groaned. That, at least, was true. "Are you OK?"

"Don't worry about me," said Brody. He glanced away into the darkness of the trees. "I think you should find Polly though, and explain."

Rhi felt even worse than before. Her sweet-natured friend had been through so much already this summer.

The last thing Polly needed was to think Rhi would ever kiss Ollie on purpose. She was exhausted, and still a little jumpy from the strange animal-headed festival goers in the woods, but she left Brody and made her way through the trees. This wasn't a conversation she was looking forward to having, but it had to be done.

"Polly! Where are you? I want to explain! It was an accident, I swear!"

She wandered around for several minutes, calling to her friend and feeling terrible. She kept having flash memories of Polly in her hospital bed when her depression and anxiety had got the better of her. She would never forgive herself if she had put Polly's recovery in jeopardy.

"Polly!" she called, hopelessly. "Are you OK? You honestly don't have anything to worry about!"

When she had made a full circle of the trees, she heard laughter coming from the campsite. That was a good sign, right? Then why did she still feel so awkward? Making her way carefully back towards the tent, she stood for a moment behind a tree, checking that everyone was around the fire. Ollie and

Polly were sitting together, Ollie with his arm around Polly's shoulders. Lila was laughing, beside Eve and Becca, as Josh leaned back against a tree and sketched the fire-lit scene. Brody sat a little way to one side, studying his hands and occasionally joining in the chatter.

Catching the mention of her name, Rhi suddenly wished herself a hundred miles away. She backed off, hating the idea that everyone was talking about her, but it was too late. She had been spotted.

"Here she is!" Lila cried, clapping her hands as Rhi sheepishly joined them by the campfire. "You little minx! Do you often go round kissing the wrong people or is this just a touch of moon madness?"

To Rhi's acute relief, Polly was laughing along with everyone else.

"Total moon madness," she mumbled. She was glad the firelight hid her blushes. "I'm so sorry to have caused all this trouble."

"Trouble?" Ollie grinned, his arm around Polly's shoulder. "You've given me my best anecdote ever. I should be thanking you. A beautiful girl running up to me in the woods..."

Josh's eyes twinkled at Rhi through his glasses. "Can I be next?"

Lila punched Josh none too softly in the arm. "Hey!" she said, with a warning note in her voice.

Josh frowned at Lila, and rubbed his arm. "That was hard," he complained. "It was only a joke. Rhi knows that."

Rhi smiled awkwardly. She didn't like being the centre of attention at the best of times, let alone in a situation as embarrassing as this. There was a strange silence.

"Right," said Becca brightly. "I think it's time for bed." She gave a yawn so large that Rhi wondered if it was fake. "I'm turning in."

Rhi couldn't meet Ollie's eye. She busied herself with holding Brody's hand instead, and smiling at him, painfully aware of the weird atmosphere that had suddenly descended on the camp.

Ollie seemed to rouse himself. He kissed Polly, and smiled at her, and pulled her into the tent with him to get comfortable for the night. Josh was still frowning at his arm, perhaps wondering if there would be a bruise in the morning. Everyone seemed uncomfortable, although there was plenty of sudden bright conversation about whether they would be able to sleep through the constant throb of the drums and what they would do in the morning. Rhi crawled into the tent on Brody's heels, wriggled into her sleeping bag, and lay in misery on her thin sleeping mat. She felt Brody settle himself silently down beside her.

"Weird day," said Eve.

"Good though," said Becca.

"Depends how you define good," Eve yawned. "Weirdo fortune tellers, lumpy bed, beans for dinner—"

"No one ever said it would be the Ritz, OK?"

There was a strange, sharp tone in Becca's voice that made Rhi want to zip her sleeping bag right up over her head. Eve grumbled and wriggled, muttering about tree roots in the small of her back.

"... really didn't mean anything..." Polly and Ollie were whispering in the corner of the tent, and Rhi got the feeling that Polly was getting upset about the kiss again.

It was an accident, she wanted to shout. But she'd

already said that. There was no point in repeating herself.

Rhi stared up at the canvas roof over her head, feeling the uneven woodland floor through her thin sleeping mat and wishing she could just fall asleep. Over in the corner of the tent, it sounded like Josh and Lila were bickering in low, tense whispers. The happy atmosphere around the campfire earlier felt like a distant memory.

Brody propped himself up on his elbow and considered Rhi in the gloom of the tent as everyone wriggled and sighed and showed no sign of drifting into a comfortable sleep. He stroked her hair back from her face, and kissed her lightly on the lips. It might have been Rhi's heightened emotions, but she sensed something tentative in the pressure of his mouth.

"Night then," he said after a moment.

Rhi lay in the dark, listening to the sounds of the forest outside the tent flaps. Maybe in the morning, everything would be back to normal.

Maybe.

EIGHT

Rhi wasn't sure what woke her. It took her a couple of groggy seconds to remember where she was. Then, turning over in her sleeping bag, she felt the hardness of the woodland floor through her sleeping mat, and remembered.

Beware the stranger in your midst. He brings dark discord. Dark discord...

Madame Felicity's words seemed to echo in the wind rustling through the trees outside the tent. The air in the tent was thick and stale, and Rhi found herself longing for lungfuls of fresh air. Her feet were cold, and her neck ached. The drummers were still drumming, though there weren't as many now. She wondered if they ever slept. Perhaps they drummed in shifts, guarding the festival, keeping away evil spirits with their incessant rhythms. She wanted to feel safe, but she didn't. Something was hanging over her like a malevolent shadow.

Inevitably, she fell to thinking about the horrible evening that had passed. The more she tried to steer her thoughts away from the animal masks and the dreadful confusion of kissing Ollie, the thicker and more insistent they became. Why had she let herself get so freaked out? It wasn't like her to be so jumpy. The consequences had been so humiliating...

As she tried to get comfortable, striving to find something more cheerful to think about, Rhi heard a strange noise. Was it the same sound that had woken her in the first place? Chilly fingers of fear stroked down her spine. Whatever spells the drummers thought they were weaving, weren't working. Something was out there.

Wide awake now, she ran through a mental checklist of what it might be. An animal? The creaking of a tree? The wind in the branches?

There was no way she would go back to sleep now.

There it was again. A clattering noise. Rhi sat up as cold sweat beaded on her forehead. Thoughts of

Skinless Meg rose to the surface of her mind as the canvas walls of the tent shivered with strange shadows. *It's just the branches outside*, she soothed herself. *Moving around in the wind.*

She tried to focus on the movement of the branches, bowing and tossing in the wind outside. It was like a dance, she realized, the branches moving in time to the distant drums, the wind rising and falling like a melody around the whole. *Nature's song*, she thought sleepily, her eyelids beginning to droop again. Not scary. Not scary at—

Something made a deep growling sound outside the tent. Rhi's eyes flew open. She screamed. There was a burst of confusion as everyone in the tent woke up together.

"What the—"

"Who screamed?"

"What's going on?"

There was a snap, and someone flicked on a torch. The cold white light was better than the dreadful darkness, but it brought its own surprises. Her heart still racing from the shock, Rhi registered that everyone had somehow swapped places during the night.

Lila was curled up with Becca, blinking sleepily in the torchlight. Polly and Josh's hands were tangled together on top of their sleeping bags. Eve was somehow spooned around Ollie's back. Nothing Rhi was seeing or hearing made sense. Why had everyone moved around? What was going on? She felt disorientated all over again.

Brody was beside her now, putting his arms around her and stroking her back. "Shh, Rhi, it's OK," he soothed. "Did you have a bad dream?"

Rhi clung gratefully to him. Her teeth were chattering so loudly, it was a miracle she could make herself heard. "There's something outside the tent!" she gasped. "An animal, something like that. It growled right by my ear!"

Everyone fell silent. And listened.

"Nothing out there," said Eve after a moment. She registered Lila and Becca curled up together on the far side of the tent and frowned. "What are you doing with Lila, Becs?"

"I might say the same thing about you and Ollie," Becca shot back. Her short chestnut hair was sticking straight up in the air.

"You didn't kiss me too, did you Eve?" laughed Ollie.

Polly paled in horror, registering the way Eve and Ollie were curled up together.

Catching his girlfriend's expression, it was clear that Ollie was already regretting his attempt at a joke. He shuffled away from Eve. "What?" he said, squirming under Polly's gaze. "I moved in my sleep, OK? That's all!"

Polly pulled her sleeping bag up to her chin and said nothing. The atmosphere grew charged.

"I date girls these days, Polly," said Eve into the silence. "In case you've forgotten."

"How many girls, exactly Eve?" Becca said in a dangerous voice.

Eve rolled her eyes at Becca's flash of jealousy. "One, last time I looked," she said pointedly. "Although that could change at any time. Polly, all I'm trying to say is that nothing happened."

"I feel like I've been hearing that a lot lately," Polly said in a small voice.

"Why are you holding Polly's hand, Josh?" Lila suddenly demanded.

"He's not!" Polly protested. "Josh wouldn't..." She stopped and stared at the way her fingers were tangled through Josh's. Josh quickly pulled his hand away. "Oh," Polly said, a little feebly.

"What's going on?" Brody asked with a big yawn.

"This is Madame Felicity's fault," said Polly anxiously. Her hazel eyes were very large in the torchlight. "She's done something strange to us all!"

Rhi agreed with Polly. Ever since they'd seen Madame Felicity, odd things had been happening. The atmosphere of this festival was like nothing she'd ever experienced, and she wasn't sure she liked it. And now this.

"I did hear something outside," she said again, a little plaintively.

"Well, it's gone away now." Brody was trying not to sound irritated. No one liked being woken up in the middle of the night for no good reason. Rhi flushed as he turned over in his sleeping bag.

"I *wasn't* holding Polly's hand," Josh said loudly from the other side of the tent. "Listen to yourself, Lila, you sound like a lunatic."

"What do you call tangling fingers then?" Lila said

crossly. Her hair was tangled, her eyes smudgy with sleep. "And you made that joke about kissing Rhi. Are you going off me or something?"

Eve settled back in her sleeping bag. "Lila," she groaned, "can't this wait until the morning? I want to go back to sleep."

"If I want to argue with my boyfriend it's no one's business but my own," Lila flared.

"Leave Lila alone, Eve," Becca snapped.

"I can have a go at Lila if I want to," said Eve, narrowing her grey eyes at her girlfriend.

Becca laughed sourly. "Is Lila the next in line to be one of your 'girls'?"

The situation was going downhill fast. Josh and Lila were still hissing at each other like angry geese. Eve and Becca were rapidly heading in the same direction. Polly watched Ollie and Eve with troubled eyes. *How has this happened?* Rhi thought, aghast.

"You are unbelievable—"

"I wish we'd never come to this stupid festival—"

"AOOOO!"

There it was again. Another creepy, throbbing howl, not far from their tent. Everyone froze. Rhi's skin prickled with dread. Was it the torchlight, or did everyone suddenly look chalk-white?

"You all heard that," Rhi gulped. "Right? I didn't imagine it?"

Polly screamed and buried her face in Ollie's shoulder.

"I can't believe how spooked we all are," said Ollie with an uneasy laugh, patting Polly gently. "I bet it was a fox, or a badger, or something like that. They scream sometimes, don't they?"

Josh cleared his throat. "Or maybe it was a car, out on the road?"

"That was no car," said Eve ominously.

"Don't worry about it," said Brody. Rhi could hear a tiny shake in his normally calm voice that did nothing to ease her fears. "It's probably just a bunch of festival goers having a laugh."

"At a quarter to four in the morning?" said Becca.

"AAOOOOOO!"

Lila screamed this time. Everyone huddled together tightly in the middle of the tent, rigid with fear, as the sound died away and a dark shadow took its place, oozing across the canvas like a pool of ink.

NINE

Everyone reached for each other in a scramble of loud panic. Fear was clogging Rhi's veins, making it impossible to think or act rationally. It was just them and whatever was out there. *Skinless Meg.*

The shadow was stretching right across the tent now. Josh dived inside his sleeping bag, and Ollie folded his arms tightly around Polly's shivering shoulders. Rhi reached for Brody, wordless with terror, grateful for his warmth and solidity.

"It won't be anything to worry about," Brody said, stroking Rhi's back a little unsteadily. "We all have overactive imaginations tonight." Through his shirt, Rhi could hear his heart beating as hard as her own. He was as unnerved as she was, Rhi realized.

The shadow moved away. Now all Rhi could see through Brody's tight embrace were the branches of the trees above their tent, moving in their familiar moonlight dance.

"This is ridiculous," said Ollie, gently prising Polly's arms away from around his waist. "I'm going out there to see what's going on."

"Don't," said Polly, her voice high with panic.

"It won't be anything scary. Everyone would feel better if they knew what it was, right?"

"So much better," Lila said fervently. "Ollie, you're a superstar."

Ollie tucked the torch between his teeth and moved on his hands and knees towards the mouth of the tent as Josh peered out of his sleeping bag. Rhi could tell he didn't like the admiring tone in Lila's voice.

"Go with him, Josh," said Lila, giving her boyfriend a prod.

Josh looked extremely unwilling. He gazed at Ollie, who was now putting on his boots. Lila was staring at him, narrow-eyed.

Josh sighed. "Fine, I'll come too. Anyone else?"

"I'm in," said Brody in his usual calm tones.

The cold night air gusted into the tent as the three boys headed out.

Becca found a second torch and switched it on. "Maybe I ought to go with them," she said. She started getting to her hands and knees. "Girl power and all that."

"You're going nowhere," Eve ordered, pulling Becca back. "The rest of us are all staying right here until they come back with a perfectly rational explanation for that noise and that shadow."

"You don't suppose..."

Lila trailed away. The others looked at her.

"What?" said Polly. Rhi worried that her friend was on the brink of a panic attack, judging from the way her fingers were clenching at the edges of her sleeping bag.

"Nothing," said Lila.

"Spit it out," said Eve impatiently.

Lila smoothed her hair back. "Madame Felicity's prediction," she said.

The tension in the tent ratcheted up again. The boy's face shimmered in Rhi's mind.

"The stranger that she mentioned." Lila lowered

her voice significantly. "What if this is connected to him and the dark discord he's going to bring?"

Polly moaned and clutched a little more tightly at her sleeping bag. Rhi didn't think she could feel any more frightened than she already did, but there it was. A cold, clenching feeling right in her gut. She wished more than anything that they'd never visited the fortune teller in her odd little caravan.

"What cheese do you use to lure a bear out of a cave?" Eve said unexpectedly.

Rhi blinked. "What?"

Lila, Becca and Polly all looked confused by Eve's question.

"It's a joke." Eve wrapped her hands around her knees. "Those ghost stories earlier scared us. It's logical that jokes will cheer us up again. So. What cheese do you use to lure a bear out of a cave?"

Rhi felt slightly less anxious. The absurdity of thinking about cheese on the most frightening night of her life was strangely soothing. "Cheddar," she said.

Lila gave a small giggle. "What's Cheddar got to do with bears, Rhi?"

74

"It was the first cheese I thought of," Rhi admitted, which made Lila guffaw.

"We give up," Becca said after a few more random guesses.

"Camembert," Eve pronounced in triumph.

Rhi laughed at that. So did Polly.

"That's the worst joke I've ever heard," said Becca, shaking her head.

"I liked it." Polly's voice sounded a little stronger. "Tell another one."

They told a few more jokes, huddling as close together in the middle of the tent as they could. It helped, but not for long. Rhi had a nasty feeling that their torch was running out of batteries. The bright torch face was definitely getting dimmer.

"I wish the boys would come back," said Polly a little plaintively. She glanced at the tent flap. "Why are they taking so long?"

"Maybe we should go and look for them," said Lila.

"Good thinking," said Becca with a nod. "There's nothing worse than sitting around and wondering what's going on. We should all get out there and take a look for ourselves. The boys might be in trouble and need rescuing."

"Becca's right," said Polly bravely. "This is the twenty-first century. We don't have to leave this to the boys."

"I'm not leaving this tent without a plan," said Eve at once. "Anything could be out there. I'll come, but only if we're prepared."

Rhi felt a wave of relief at the suggestion that they should go out and hunt for the boys. She didn't think she could stand another five minutes of waiting.

The girls hunted through their rucksacks for weapons that they could take with them. Rhi wondered if there were some tools in the van, but as it was parked some distance away, she quickly abandoned that idea and took up the wooden spoon Becca had used to cook the veggie stew. Polly gave a few experimental swipes in the air with her hairbrush. Becca handed out tins of baked beans that they could throw if needed. Eve produced a large can of hairspray from the bottom of her bag.

"What are you going to do, style your attacker to death?" Lila scoffed, pulling on her boots. "'Hi, I'm a crazed bear with a taste for human flesh and I'm having a really bad fur day. Could you please give me a makeover?'"

"Clearly, you've never had a hairspray accident," said Eve. She studied Lila's dark mop of hair with disapproval. "I get it in my eyes all the time. Believe me, it's extremely painful. Rhi, you can take the hairspray. I have a pair of high-heeled shoes which will inflict serious damage if thrown at the correct angle."

"You brought high-heeled shoes to a festival in the woods?" said Becca, startled.

"They're at least two seasons old," Eve said, as if that explained it. "The heels are really quite ugly."

Rhi felt a giggle rising in her throat as she took the silver can Eve was passing to her. Giggling was good. It pushed away any residual fear.

"We should agree a call that we'll all recognize." Becca's face looked animated in the fading torchlight. Rhi could tell she was starting to enjoy herself. "An owl or something. So if we hear it, we know someone's in trouble."

"I hate to burst your bubble, Becs, but it's night-time, and we're in a wood," Eve said kindly.

77

"There are probably hundreds of owls in these trees already."

Becca looked disappointed.

"Three claps," Polly suggested. "Clapping isn't something you normally hear in a wood. And," she added, "clapping feels like a cheerful, safe thing to do. You know what I mean?"

"Three claps it is," Eve said with a brisk nod. "And no calling out, OK? There are people trying to sleep."

They dressed quickly, tucking their weapons in their pockets, and started crawling towards the tent flaps. Lila reached for the zip and prepared to yank it downwards.

A huge shadow blocked out the moonlight that had been dappling the canvas roof.

"AAOOOOO!"

Polly screamed. Eve almost toppled backwards, right into Becca. Rhi reached frantically for the hairspray in her pocket as the dark shadow spread . . . and spread. . . Now the shadow was taking shape, she could see that it was tall. . . Were those spikes on its head? How many arms did it have? *The rattle of a toe-bone necklace. . .*

78

The girls stared, transfixed, as the zipper slowly started to lower. Rhi forced her hands to move, levelling her can of hairspray at the flaps as something huge came crashing into the tent.

"AAOOO! *AAOOOOO!*"

TEN

Rhi had the brief sense of a creature with strange green scales that seemed to shine in the torchlight. Its branch-like arms were held out so wide that they touched the sides of the tent. Polly and Lila were screaming like banshees, and even Eve and Becca had temporarily lost all power of speech.

"AAOOOO!" the creature howled, advancing closer.

Becca found her voice. With a warlike cry, she charged at the monster. There was a muffled thud as the green figure was knocked to the groundsheet, followed by the ungainly sound of scuffling.

Rhi pressed her finger hard on the hairspray button, straight towards where she imagined the creature's face to be, somewhere near the top of its shaggy green body as it writhed around on the ground. *Whhhshshshtt!* The tent filled with the choking smell of chemicals.

"AAOOO—*ooowww*!"

The creature's throaty roar changed noticeably to something that sounded like the yells of a human in pain.

The smell of hairspray seemed to spur Eve, Lila and Polly into action.

"Get it, Becs!" Eve screeched as Becca rolled around the tent with her arms wrapped grimly around her quarry.

Polly started lobbing high-heeled shoes and baked-bean tins. The missiles ricocheted off the canvas walls, forcing Rhi to shield herself with her rucksack, and hit the monster with a satisfying series of *crack*s.

"Ow ow ow! What the— what *is* this stuff, it's in my eyes..."

"I've been stabbed! I've been—"

"Stop it! OW!"

The creature's head collapsed in on itself thanks to one particularly well-aimed baked-bean tin from Polly. Leaves, twigs and pine needles showered to the ground and Ollie was revealed, frantically rubbing the back of his head with his hands.

"Help!" Ollie groaned, trying to ward off the fresh volley of shoes and hairbrushes. "OW!"

More twigs and leaves fell away, revealing Josh and Brody trying to hide themselves behind Ollie. The monster's branch-like arms *were* branches, Rhi realized, wielded by Josh, who was now holding them above his head as a makeshift shield much in the same way she had wielded the rucksack.

"Hit them harder, Poll!" Lila yelled, and Polly furiously walloped the back end of the leaf-covered monster with her hairbrush.

"OW!" Ollie roared again.

Brody lay in the middle of the tent, holding his stomach and laughing uproariously, still covered in a thin coating of leaves and pine needles. Rhi sprayed him with a long blast of hairspray, furious and scared and relieved all at the same time.

"Brody, you... I can't believe you..."

"It was just a joke!" he choked, trying to protect himself from the sticky, stinking spray. "Chill out, will you?"

Josh leaped into the air with a shout of pain at a well-aimed shoe heel from Eve. Lila had run out of tins, and was whirling around the tent in a blur of furiously thumping arms and legs. In a final gesture of fury, Polly threw her hairbrush straight at Ollie, and missed. The brush went spinning towards the open tent flap and disappeared into the night with a thump.

The noise seemed to bring everyone to their senses. No one was fighting monsters any more. They were just in a tent, in the middle of the night, breathing heavily and staring at each other.

The boys stood up cautiously, brushing off the last remaining leaves. Eve stalked across the tent to retrieve her shoes, and look a little sadly at the empty hairspray can that had rolled into one corner. Lila and Becca both sank to the ground, shaking their heads wordlessly.

"Joke?" Ollie offered feebly into the silence.

"Look at this MESS!" Polly wailed, pressing her hands to her cheeks. "Who's going to clear it up?"

Their tent seemed to contain half the forest. Leaves were everywhere. Branches lay at strange angles across the sleeping bags. Pine needles spread over everything like a fine green dust.

"Three names spring to mind," Rhi said pointedly.

The boys had the grace to blush as Eve, Becca, Polly and Lila folded their arms and stared at them alongside Rhi.

"You are *so* cleaning this up," Lila growled.

"Don't even try to wriggle out of it," Eve added.

Becca tapped the palm of her hand with one of Eve's shoes in a meaningful way.

"I think we're beaten, guys," Josh grinned.

"OK, so it was a bad joke," admitted Ollie.

"It was a great joke," said Brody, laughing. "Only we got the worst of it."

"See what happens when you send me out in the middle of the night with these two maniacs?" Josh told Lila, thumbing at Ollie and Brody.

Lila seemed to swell like a balloon. "So this is *my* fault, is it?"

Josh seemed to realize he was on dangerous ground. He backtracked at once. "No," he said cautiously. "I guess it's not."

Becca pointed the shoe dangerously at Ollie. "The three of you are going to clean up *every last pine needle* in this tent, OK?"

84

"Message received loud and clear," said Ollie with a sigh. "Come on, guys. If we're quick, we might all get back to sleep by sunrise."

Rhi and the others sat outside and left the boys to tidy up. The moonlit woodland was quiet and still after the chaos of the monster fight. Rhi glimpsed the spreading wings of an owl as it swooped silently on a vole in the undergrowth. Nature, savage and beautiful, wild and peaceful all at the same time. *No wonder we have been feeling so strange*, she mused. *Humans don't really belong in the woods at night at all.*

"Idiots," Lila muttered every few minutes. "And I bet they never even looked for the real howling thing."

"We did look," Josh shouted from inside the tent. "But we swear there was nothing. It must have been an animal and some trick of the moonlight."

"I'm sure Josh is right," Eve said. It sounded to Rhi like she was trying to convince herself. "It's a very bright moon tonight and the woods are full of animals you never see in the daytime."

"I still think it was Madame Felicity," Polly said, sounding stubborn about it.

Rhi wished she could believe Josh, but she couldn't.

The howling sound had been unearthly, unlike any animal sound she'd ever heard. Plus the shadow had been too long and thin to be an animal. Was the woodland telling them that they weren't welcome? She wondered uneasily if they'd ever find out the truth. The night distorted things...

Brody carried out an armful of branches and dumped them beside the cold campfire. "Firewood for tomorrow at least," he joked, but the girls gazed stonily at him and he quickly returned to the tent.

Rhi lay back on the leafy woodland floor and stared up at the moon, which was high in the sky and shining with full force into their camping glade. A few clouds drifted by, but the light that it cast was almost as bright as day. Part of her wanted to sleep right where she lay, but the rest of her was still too jumpy. She wished the boys had looked a little harder.

The clock was approaching five a.m. by the time everyone crawled back inside and got into their sleeping bags again. And still the drums played, thumping dreamily in the forest.

"Tomorrow I'm going put my foot through every drum that I see," Eve growled.

"I find it kind of soothing," Becca yawned.

"Idiots," Lila hissed at the boys one last time.

Brody snuggled up to Rhi, kissing her apologetically on the back of the neck. Rhi let him, glad of his presence but still too wired for sleep.

It wasn't long before the tent filled with steady breathing. The shadows changed on the tent from moment to moment, but there was no sign of the strange, thin shadow returning. For a few blessed moments, the drums fell silent. An owl seemed to hoot in celebration. Rhi lay where she was, still wide awake.

"What a night," she grumbled, gazing at the canvas roof.

There was no reply.

ELEVEN

Rhi's eyes felt gritty. Rubbing her face with her palms, she stared at the cluster of pine needles that came off on her fingers.

"Why didn't you tell me my face was green?" she complained.

Brody glanced up from absently tuning his guitar. "Can't say I noticed," he confessed.

Rhi whacked him, but not too hard. The antics of the previous night were more or less forgiven. Ollie and Polly had wandered off to find the Chakra Café an hour earlier, both yawning so widely it was amazing they could see where they were going. Josh had persuaded Lila to pose for a sketch on the Oak Horse; he had promised to frame the result and give it to her as a way of saying sorry. Eve had been scoping out the beautiful henna designs on many of the festival goers' arms and legs the previous day, so Rhi guessed that's where she and Becca were. Which just left her and Brody, sitting by the relit campfire and practising their set for the afternoon's gig.

"We'll be on time for the gig, don't worry," Lila had promised, as Josh had dragged her away through the guy ropes with his sketch pad under his arm. "Wouldn't miss it. Besides, you'll need our pedal power for the songs, won't you? *Ow*, Josh, stop *pulling* me, I'm going as fast as I can..."

Stifling a yawn with her hand, Rhi crawled back inside the tent, retrieved her pillow and gave it a good shake by the campfire. A shower of pine needles rained on Brody's head, trickling down the neck of his T-shirt.

"Now you can itch for a while," she said, enjoying the way he squirmed. "See how you like it. What's the time?"

"We still have an hour before we perform. I think we should run through 'Heartbreaker' again. The tuning was a little out first time through."

It always felt strange, singing "Heartbreaker" with Brody. Rhi had written it when she was going through a difficult time with her ex-boyfriend Max. Brody played it beautifully, but it felt odd to hear the words on his lips.

"Heartbreaker, lead me astray... Heartbreaker, show me a way..."

Rhi wished she knew the way through the confusion in her own head. Thoughts of Madame Felicity hadn't faded with the night, as she'd hoped they would. *Do not confuse the muse with love...* Was she going to break Brody's heart? Was he going to break hers? She sang the harmonies, trying to keep pace with Brody's playing, but she was so tired... She found her thoughts wandering to wooden caravans and glowing hair and she missed a couple of easy entries.

They tried Brody's new song next. Rhi felt the old lurch of dread as she remembered the words. How they suggested that she and Brody...

"The rhythms are dancing, the harmonies too, the music in me and the music in you," Brody sang. "The music in me ... and the music in—"

90

"Do we have to do that song?" Rhi blurted without thinking.

Brody stopped playing at once. "I thought you liked it." He sounded hurt.

Rhi rushed to reassure him. "It's beautiful, Brody, really. I just... I'm not completely confident about performing it in public yet."

Brody shrugged. "Fine. What do you want to do instead?"

"'Small Black Box'?"

"Small Black Box" had strange connotations too, Rhi realized, as they sang through their new song about secrets.

"Got a small black box, locked up tight, hidden the key deep in the night – a small black box, buried down deep... Sometimes there's secrets you just have to keep."

Rhi saw partway through the final verse that Brody was tutting over the strings. "I can never get that progression right," he muttered.

Brody wasn't his usual chilled-out self, Rhi realized. Was something bothering him, or was it just the result of a bad night's sleep? Her reaction just now to his new song – the one he'd written for her – probably hadn't helped. She wanted to talk to him about how he was feeling, but didn't know how.

"Can we do that bit again?" said Brody with a sigh.

"A small black box, buried down deep," Rhi sang obediently... "Sometimes there's secrets you just have to keep."

Brody tutted again, and struck his strings in a show of frustration. "Sorry," he said, looking up at Rhi. "It's just... I got it right back at home, it shouldn't be difficult. One more time?"

After a third attempt, Brody seemed satisfied, but still strangely tense. Rhi was about to ask him if he was OK when he jumped to his feet with a muttered oath.

"We need to go," he said. "Kristina and Gerald wanted a soundcheck before the gig starts."

Rhi felt a little rush of panic. She hadn't done her hair or make-up, or anything! After the night they'd all had, she felt sure she looked like a zombie. "You said we had time!" she said, startled and worried. "I have to change..."

"Be quick," he called after her as she wriggled into

the tent to find the outfit she'd planned specially for this gig. A short green playsuit that brought out green flecks in her eyes and matched the large green earrings she'd bought the previous week. The playsuit was a bit wrinkled but it would have to do.

Rhi snatched up her make-up bag and shoved it into her rucksack. She'd have to do her make-up backstage. "Brody!" she called plaintively, coming out of the tent again to see the back of her boyfriend's blond head already making its way through the tents towards the festival site. "*Wait*, will you?"

There was no one at the striped tent. Even the bicycle generator had disappeared. *Great*, thought Rhi, biting her lip and looking around at the crowds as they milled among the stalls and tepees and gathered in colourful groups around the Oak Horse. *Now what?*

"Yoo-hoo!" Kristina was wearing five flower garlands, her feet bare and dirty. She beamed to see Rhi and Brody. "Right on time! Change of venue, I'm afraid. I'm sorry to tell you, but this tent was pitched in *quite* the wrong spot. The ley lines are a *mess*."

Only at a New Age festival would this be important, Rhi thought, biting her lip and exchanging anxious glances with Brody. Was their gig cancelled, or did the long-haired organizer have a plan B?

"So where are we singing?" Brody prompted, as Kristina was still shaking her head at the ignorance of whoever had pitched the striped tent.

Kristina seemed surprised by the question. "The main stage, of course," she said, as if it had been the obvious answer all along.

Rhi felt a sudden rush of excitement. They had seen the main stage yesterday, with a crowd of several hundred gathered to listen to the music. The striped tent would have held fifty, maximum.

"The main stage?" Brody repeated. "Don't you have another act booked for that?"

"The Oak Horse saw fit to strike this afternoon's act down with a stomach upset so our path is clear." Kristina smiled warmly at them. "The main stage is set most carefully at the convergence of five ley lines. *Quite* the energy portal. Follow me!"

They passed campfires, drummers and a totem pole that had popped up overnight, before reaching the main stage: a large structure with a rainbow-coloured awning and pennants fluttering from the top like

94

something from King Arthur's court. A smaller, open-sided tent towards the trees housed three bicycles, all connected to a generator behind the stage. Rhi started to relax and enjoy the sensation of being in the heart of things. She quickly did her make-up backstage and then helped Brody as he tuned his guitar and directed the gathering crowd on to the bicycles that would power the amps. She loved performing with him so much.

"Hey there, Oak Horse," said Brody into the microphone. "Are you ready to rock?"

"Fast Lane Freak" took off a little slower than usual. Rhi felt an unusual thump of adrenaline as she tried to slow herself down to Brody's pace. The crowd had their arms in the air, flags and pennants waving.

"Trash and cash is all the same, everybody ride that gravy train, breathe the fumes and breathe the fame..."

There was something slightly off about Brody's performance. Rhi couldn't put her finger on it, but as they moved through the set she found it harder and harder to tune herself to him. They usually matched each other, note for note, both feeling the music on what Rhi could only describe as a soul level – but today was different. Today was hard work. Rhi hoped this strange loss of connection was a simple case of exhaustion. She felt sure Brody was just as tired as she was.

Rhi took a break at the back of the stage as Brody sang his solo ballad, "Be With Me". Spotting Ollie and the others waving at her from the bicycles, she was relieved to see them. It would have been the last straw if their friends had missed the gig altogether.

"Be with me, lie with me, die with me, for ever," Brody sang, quietly, leaning into the microphone with his eyes closed. "Be with me, lie with me, die with me, for ever..."

Rhi could see their tent beyond the swaying crowd, way back in the trees. She recognized the fluttering pennant that Eve had attached to the roof. Madame Felicity's caravan would be somewhere along to the right. She let her eyes trail through the trees, looking for the little green wagon on wheels, the tiny horse, but there was no sign.

She looked again. The caravan had definitely been there last night; she recognized the large red tent in the foreground, and the big oak tree where Madame Felicity had strung out her clothes line. She really wasn't there. Today was the biggest day of the Oak Horse festival. Plenty of business. Why hadn't she stuck around?

I wish I'd never met her, Rhi thought irritably. *She's brought me nothing but confusion.*

TWELVE

For the rest of the set, Rhi had the same unsettling feeling of being out of step with her musical partner. To the untrained ear, she and Brody sounded great: their lyrics were as catchy as ever, the harmonies glorious, and Brody's playing was at its best. The crowd went wild at the end of pretty much every song, with Rhi's friends screaming and clapping the loudest. And yet... Rhi couldn't help feeling that she was following Brody instead of running beside him. Trying to keep up on unfamiliar paths, tree roots all around threatening to trip her up.

They encored with "Sundown, Sunshine" with its thundering, catchy riff. Rhi realized with a delicious shock that several groups in the crowd – people she'd never met – already knew the words. They must have researched her and Brody's songs on the internet. It was an intoxicating feeling.

"Be my sundown, Sunshine, my sundown, run-up-to-sun-up Sunshine," she sang beside Brody.

"My moonrise, my night skies, my twilight, my all-night, my turn-off-the-light, my Sunshine, be mine, be mine," the crowd responded, waving flags and dancing. "My Sunshine, be mine!"

Rhi felt Brody break off the song a fraction of a second before she did. The odd disconnect she had felt between them all morning was back. *I have to know why.*

"Something's the matter," she said abruptly. "Isn't it?"

"Bow now, talk later," Brody hissed.

Rhi bowed and waved, the crowd shrieking its approval, her mind wholly on the boy beside her. She tugged Brody off the stage at the first opportunity.

"Talk to me," she said, as people backstage smiled and nodded approval and handed them bottles of water.

Brody spent a while fiddling with the strings of his guitar. Then he slung it over his shoulder and looked Rhi square in the eye.

"I didn't like seeing you kiss Ollie."

I knew it, Rhi thought. Brody had acted cool at the time, but it had clearly bothered him. She felt panicky. "I told you that was a mistake!"

"I still didn't like seeing it," he repeated. "Our musical connection is strong, Rhi. No one denies that, least of all me. But this weird jealousy thing I've been feeling all day... I don't know. It's messed with my head. And it's messed with our music."

"It won't happen again," Rhi insisted helplessly. "It was a weird night."

Brody took her hand. "I don't want to lose what we have," he said. "I feel like we lost it up there today."

"I know what you mean," Rhi whispered. She gripped Brody's fingers. "I don't want to lose it either."

Do not confuse the muse with love. Madame Felicity was back, drifting through Rhi's mind, her long purple nails curled like claws. The things Brody was saying were eerily close to the fortune teller's prediction.

Brody kissed her gently on the lips. "We'll work it out. Let's find the others," he said.

Ollie, Polly, Josh, Eve, Lila and Becca were all

waiting by the foot of the stage. Rhi was temporarily lifted out of her gloom at the sight of Eve, whose arms were painted with intricate henna designs.

"Wow, Eve, did you turn into a hippy today?" Rhi teased, as their friends crowded around them with hoots of celebration and warm hugs.

Eve angled her arms to admire them a little better. "I think it's rather fun. I wanted Becca to get one done as well, but she said she was too ticklish."

"What?" Becca said, blushing a little as everyone laughed. "It's true, I can't bear the feeling of little brushes on my skin. That's totally normal, as far as I'm concerned."

Rhi realized she was starving. They loaded up on falafels at one of the food stalls, and sat down in the shade of the Oak Horse to eat them. They were delicious: hot, spicy and fragrant.

"I hope these weren't to blame for that band's stomach upsets," Brody remarked as they munched their food in the cool grass.

Rhi patted the long wooden leg of the Oak Horse beside her. "According to Kristina, it was the fault of this guy, not the falafels," she said.

"The spirit of the Oak Horse is strong," Ollie intoned, waving his arms in a suitably hippyish way.

"You speak the truth, friend!" someone shouted nearby, waving his arms in agreement. "The Oak Horse lives in us all!"

Everyone collapsed into uncontrollable giggles at the look on Ollie's face. "I wasn't serious," he protested. "I didn't think anyone was listening!"

"The Oak Horse is listening right now," Eve said, smirking. "And he's about to kick you clean across this festival with one massive hoof."

"Imagine the splinters," Josh added, which set Lila off again.

They hung out in the heart of the festival for the rest of the afternoon. Rhi and Brody were stared at, and smiled at, and Rhi heard snatches of their songs as they walked by. *I could get used to this*, she thought, warmed by the air of appreciation. They joined a t'ai chi workshop, and though she protested that she didn't really believe in it, Polly had her birth chart read. Becca was persuaded to get three colourful threaded braids put in her chestnut hair. Josh found endless artists to talk to and share his work with; so much so that Lila lost him on three occasions.

The sun dipped below the trees. As well as the bands on the main stage, there were zither players, a guy with an electric fiddle and a whole orchestra of bottle-top blowers. Rhi tried her hand at bottle-top blowing, but her friends made her laugh too much for it to be a success. They danced until they were drenched with sweat, and Eve lost a shoe in the press around the main stage. The fire-eaters came out with the night, walking tall on long stilts as they blew light and sparks into the night air. The Oak Horse watched it all, tall and impassive throughout.

Rhi had no idea what the time was. All she knew was that she was exhausted. The thought of her sleeping bag and tent was getting ever more tempting. But the darkness and the shadows were starting to remind her of the previous evening, and the last thing she wanted was to return to the tent by herself. What if she got lost again? She pictured the strangers in their animal masks, and remembering the curious howl, shuddered.

She tugged Brody away from where he was dancing with Lila.

"Walk me back?" she pleaded.

It turned out everyone was happy to return to the tent. Last night's broken sleep was catching up with all of them as well.

"Great night," Eve yawned, her arm wrapped sleepily around Becca's waist. "We're staying in a hotel tonight, right?"

"You wish," said Becca, grinning. Her colourful hair braids bobbed around her face. They suited her.

"We'll all sleep like babies," Ollie declared.

"Yelling for food every couple of hours and wetting the bed," Josh added, which made Lila laugh sleepily.

Rhi was finding it hard to put one foot in front of the other, she was so tired. Brody was walking faster than she would have liked, and she had to put on an extra burst of effort to keep up. *I can't get lost. Not again.*

The trees pressed around them. Still chatting and laughing, the others moved onwards, oblivious to the feelings of dread that were beginning to freeze Rhi's veins.

A flash of silver caught her eye, away to the left of the path they were on. Rhi stopped dead, and stared. A figure was drifting through the trees. Tall, with long glowing hair... Rhi rubbed her eyes and stared again, her heart in her mouth. *A trick of the moonlight, it's just a trick...* But it wasn't a trick, she could see it clearly. It was Madame Felicity, transparent somehow, the moonlight glowing through her...

Rhi gasped loudly, transfixed. Brody turned.

"What?"

Rhi couldn't speak. She simply pointed wordlessly at the figure – only the figure wasn't there anymore. A shaft of moonlight glowed mockingly where Madame Felicity had been standing moments earlier.

"What?" said Eve, suddenly by Rhi's side and looking alert. "Did you see something?"

"A g— A g—" Rhi couldn't get the words out. No one would believe her, no one ever believed her...

"Rhi, you're freaking us out here," said Ollie as the others crowded uneasily around, peering into the trees, trying to see whatever it was that Rhi was pointing at.

"A ghost!" Rhi managed finally to babble. "I saw a *ghost*!"

"Excellent!" said Ollie cheerfully. "More ghost stories."

"I'm serious! I... It was... I swear I saw..."

Becca put her arm around Rhi's shoulders. "We're all really tired," she said gently. "Come on, Rhi, the tent's not much further."

Rhi took one look at her friends' faces and knew. They all thought she was completely mad.

THIRTEEN

Madame Felicity's ghost, real or imagined, seemed to hang over the tent for the rest of the night. Rhi tossed and turned, flushing with humiliation every time she thought about the way her friends had looked at each other when she had babbled on about seeing the figure among the trees. She was unable to get to sleep. Beside her, she could sense Brody was sleepless as well. She found that she didn't want to talk to him. She wasn't sure why. Perhaps it was because of their half-concluded conversation backstage, about the way their relationship seemed to be changing – and not for the better.

Was this the worst trip ever? Rhi wondered, as owls screeched out in the woods for the second sleepless night in a row. She was sticky and tired, longing for a shower, hungry and cold and uncomfortable, and horribly embarrassed. How was she going to face the others when the sun finally rose? She didn't want to think about that, so of course, it was all she *could* think about.

Rhi was beginning to wonder if the night would ever end when the first flicker of early dawn light stole into the tent. There was an unearthly scream outside. The way everyone instantly sat up told Rhi that the others had slept about as well as she had.

"Twirly," mumbled Josh, curled up in a tiny ball by the mouth of the tent.

"Josh is clearly doing pirouettes in his sleep," said Ollie grumpily. "I wish I was so lucky."

"Not 'twirly', you plonk," Lila snapped. "TOO EARLY. What *is* that? Doesn't anyone at this dumb festival ever sleep?"

Rhi felt a flicker of miserable anger. *Everyone's here having the worst time ever, and it's all my fault. Now I can add guilt to my general feelings of embarrassment. Happy days.*

"I'm going to have bags under my eyes you could

carry the shopping home in," Eve croaked. "And cucumber slices are *not* going to fix them."

Becca climbed wearily out of her sleeping bag and unzipped the tent to see what was going on. Rhi peered over Becca's shoulder at the strange sight of a circle of people dancing in a nearby glade. Every now and then, one of the dancers would emit a whoop and throw themselves to the ground with a thump that made Rhi wonder about bruises.

"Great sun, give us light so we may grow like plants upon the surface of your beloved earth!" called the leader: a tiny skinny man with a long purple beard.

"Shine on us!" shouted the rest of the circle, throwing themselves to the ground again.

"Great sun, give us warmth that we might bask in your goodness!"

"Shine on us!"

"Great sun, give us gratitude for the lives that we lead!"

Polly rubbed her eyes sourly. "I don't think this is much to be grateful for. Ollie, can't you tell them to stop it?"

"Great sun, give us shadows that we might know the purity of the light!"

"Shine on us!"

Ollie wriggled past Becca, out into the waking forest. Rhi could hear him clear his throat. "Excuse me, do you have to—"

"Great sun, give us hope that we might always know your goodness!"

"Shine on us!"

Ollie tried again. "I'm sorry to disturb you, but is there any chance you can do this somewhere else? Away from our tent?"

"Great sun, give us—"

Josh sat bolt upright. "SOME OF US ARE TRYING TO SLEEP IN HERE!" he roared.

The ceremony outside stopped.

"You have to know how to talk to these people," Josh told the others with sleepy satisfaction before flopping down into his sleeping bag again.

Ollie crawled back inside the tent. Everyone exchanged relieved looks. They settled down again, though Rhi knew in her heart no one would sleep now that the sunlight was starting to filter through the canvas.

"Great sun, give us peace in our hearts that we might know that you bring life to all!"

"Oh, for goodness' sake," Eve snapped, throwing back her sleeping bag covers. "Those sun-worshipping fools sound as if they've moved precisely three trees away. How is that 'going somewhere else'? There's no point trying to sleep through this. We might as well have breakfast."

"No food," Becca mumbled.

"What?" said Ollie in dismay.

"We're out of food," Becca repeated. "Someone's been eating more than their fair share this weekend."

"Don't look at me," Ollie objected, looking offended as everyone stared at him. "I haven't been eating more than anyone else."

"You haven't exactly been sharing your private stock of salami though, have you?" Brody observed a little caustically.

"I need meat," Ollie spluttered. "You might be able to survive on the rabbit food you can get in this stupid place, but I can't."

"You didn't have to come with us," said Polly, sounding stung.

"Maybe you should have told me that on Friday," Ollie said sourly. "I'm missing a whole weekend of football training for this."

"*Ollie!*"

Rhi didn't think she'd ever heard Polly get angry with Ollie before. The atmosphere in the tent was getting ugly.

After a couple more restless hours of semi-sleep and a thin breakfast of stale bread and fragments of leftover cheese, Rhi and the others tried to relight the campfire to boil a pan of water. But there had been heavy dewfall in the night and the twigs refused to catch.

"That's all we need," Ollie complained. "No breakfast and now no coffee."

Josh pulled on his boots and went to check out the food situation in the festival site. The others sat glumly around the cold campfire, waiting for him to return, while Ollie fantasized loudly about bacon sandwiches.

They waited for over an hour for Josh to come back.

"He's found something interesting to draw and forgotten about us," Ollie grumbled.

"Maybe the food stalls aren't open yet," said Polly.

Polly was absolutely right. Josh returned, annoyed and hungry, with nothing to show for his trip but a hat full of freshly picked blackberries.

"All the food stalls were shut up," he said as he put his hat down by the fire. "But I found a big bramble bush behind the main stage."

"They aren't washed," said Eve doubtfully as she looked at the glistening berries.

Josh glared. "A thank you would be nice. I pricked my fingers a *lot* to get these."

The atmosphere didn't improve as they ate the blackberries. Josh looked irritably at the berry stain in his hat before cramming it back on his head. Eve and Lila went back to their sleeping bags. Brody leaned back against the nearest tree and practised his guitar. The songs that he picked sounded melancholy to Rhi's ears.

At ten o'clock, Ollie announced he would eat the main stage if the food stalls still weren't open. His temper wasn't improved by Eve and Lila taking ages to get ready. Becca looked fretfully up into the patch of sky above their forest glade as everyone finally assembled outside the tent, ready to venture on to the festival site.

"What?" said Rhi, following Becca's gaze.

"I think it's going to rain," she said.

Everyone heard the rumble of thunder. Within moments, it seemed to Rhi, the sky darkened to the colour of gunmetal and the rain began to fall in great heavy sheets, soaking them all within moments.

"Take cover!" Josh shouted over the loud drumming of the rain.

Polly and Ollie dived for the tent, colliding with Lila and Josh at the door. Stumbling forward, hopelessly off balance, Polly crashed into Ollie and ricocheted into one of the main tent poles, bringing it down with her. As Lila's foot slipped on the wet groundsheet, she and Josh tipped headlong into the canvas, with Josh's foot wrapping itself around a guy rope and pulling it out of the ground. Eve shrieked in the heart of the tangle, Becca tried to pull Josh upright, and Brody and Rhi were both caught up in the wet and flailing chaos as the entire tent collapsed in a billowing mass.

"My clothes!" Lila shouted. "My stuff! Urgh, I'm *drenched*. Polly, you are useless!"

"Don't call her useless!" Ollie shouted back, flailing in the tangle of ropes as Polly stammered apologies to anyone who would listen. "If you hadn't taken so long to get ready..."

"If you hadn't eaten all the food we wouldn't have had to wait for Josh to come back with those horrible berries..."

"I didn't see you complaining when you were eating them!"

Rhi did her best to calm everyone down, but it was no good. The rain was falling harder, the group was getting wetter, and tempers had been well and truly lost.

"This is all Madame Felicity's fault," Polly wept. "We should never have come here."

"Will you just shut up about that stupid fortune teller?" Ollie snarled. "We have bigger problems right now—"

"*You're* the problem, Ollie!" Lila said, panting with rage. "Madame Felicity was right, she knew things. She knew I was a free spirit, she said I had to stay free..."

"Sounds like I'm being dumped," said Josh shortly.

"Lila!" said Rhi, horrified by the direction this

argument seemed to be taking. "We said we wouldn't tell the boys about the predicti—" She stopped dead as the boys looked at her.

"What did she tell you, Rhi?" Brody asked.

"That you and her aren't supposed to be together, OK?" Lila was in full spate now and wouldn't be stopped. "Don't deny it Rhi, we were all there. We all heard it. And Eve and Becca – you can forget it too, can't you?"

Eve and Becca both turned white as sheets at Lila's pronouncement.

"Am I being dumped or not?" Josh demanded. "Why didn't you mention this prediction, Lila? Don't storm off…"

But Lila had pulled free from the tangled tent and was running towards the festival site. Josh yanked his foot out of the guy ropes, snatched up his sketch pad and marched away in the opposite direction.

Ollie and Polly were arguing now. Rhi realized with a sinking heart that she was the subject.

"How could you do that to me?"

"I am sick of telling you that kiss meant nothing, Polly … it was just a crazy moment… Why am I always having to explain myself to you, why can't you take what I say at face value for once?"

"Maybe Madame Felicity was right," said Eve, staring at Becca as Polly fled, sobbing, into the trees with Ollie giving chase. "What are we doing together if this isn't going to be for ever?"

Becca made a strange choking sound, bringing her hands to her mouth before running away towards the Oak Horse, Eve stiffly extracted herself from the tangled canvas and stood up, smoothing back her hair. "I guess that's it then," she said tightly before her face crumpled into sobs and she, too, ran away.

Rhi and Brody were the only two left sitting in the middle of the soggy, collapsed tent. It was still pouring, but Rhi hardly noticed. *We haven't even met the stranger yet, and already we've destroyed ourselves,* she thought numbly.

All her friends had just broken up. Every single one of them.

FOURTEEN

"This is insane!" Rhi whispered, reeling from shock. "Everyone just split up because of a crazy fortune teller?" As the words came out of her mouth, she wished she really could dismiss Madame Felicity's predictions as easily as she pretended.

"Try telling them that," Brody sighed as he pushed his soaking hair out of his eyes.

The rain passed almost as suddenly as it had begun. Sunlight burst through the wet treetops with a dazzling effect, gleaming on the leaves and the wet trunks. Campers started to emerge cautiously from their tents. Several of the madder ones did a kind of sun dance around their smouldering campfires amid jokes and laughter. Rhi had never felt less like laughing in her life.

"We have to do something," she wailed, looking at Brody.

"Like what?"

Madame Felicity, Rhi thought. She'd started all this. She was the one to end it. "I'm going to find that fortune teller," she said.

Grabbing Brody's hand, she tried to pull him away from the wrecked campsite, to help her find the mysterious silver-haired woman that had caused such chaos.

"We can't leave the tent like this," Brody protested, pulling her back again. "We have to put it back up, tidy away, hang out the wet stuff so it can dry—"

Didn't Brody get it? Didn't he realize how serious this was? "Later," Rhi insisted. "You have to help me find Madame Felicity right now. She's the only one who can help!"

Brody sighed, but let Rhi pull him towards the festival site. "Where is she, then?"

Rhi thought of the empty site where the fortune-teller's caravan had stood on Friday night. "I don't know," she said, biting her lip. "She moved. She must be somewhere else on the site."

They started at the main stage, hunting among the tepees and bivouacs and yurts for Madame Felicity's caravan. Brody made Rhi describe it in detail.

"It was green, with this hand-painted sign on the side. The horse was piebald – white and brown. She had a campfire, and an old kettle, and a washing line... She *has* to be here somewhere!"

"Vehicles aren't allowed on the site," Brody pointed out, looking around. "We had to leave our van by the road, remember?"

Rhi hesitated. Did a horse-drawn caravan count as a vehicle? They scanned the cars parked along the sides of the festival just in case, but there was no sign of the little green house on wheels, its iron chimney sputtering out smoke.

People were starting to pack up, tents were being put away. When Rhi saw a battered hat that looked like Josh's, she spun around – but it wasn't Josh at all. Seeing the hat made her think about the rest of her friends, scattered across the festival with their broken hearts and aching souls. *This is all my fault*, she thought. *Lila was right. We should never have come to this place.*

"What are you going to do when – if – we find this

person?" Brody asked as they returned to searching the aisles, the stalls, the marquees near the main stage.

"Make her come back to the campsite with me, and tell the others that the fortunes she told them were all an act, a stupid money-making—" Rhi paused as something odd struck her.

"She's not going to do that," Brody said, half laughing. "That would be like putting a big sign on her head announcing 'I'm a fraud who's only after your money'!"

She wasn't after our money, Rhi thought in distraction. *She never asked for payment, and we never offered it. She just invited us in, and told us things. Showed us her crystal ball, and the dark boy's face...* "I'll kidnap her horse if I have to," she said aloud, shaking her head to dislodge the crazy thoughts she was having. "We have to find her and put this right, Brody!"

But no matter how hard they looked, they couldn't see Madame Felicity or her caravan anywhere. They struck out through the woods, fanning out, hunting for the old kettle, the quietly grazing horse ... but it was as if the fortune teller had never existed.

After more than an hour of hunting, Rhi sat down

on the wet grass by the Oak Horse's hooves, utterly defeated. "I don't know what else to do," she groaned, and buried her head in her hands.

Brody put his arm around her. "Hey, at least we've got one piece of good news."

"What?" said Rhi disbelievingly.

"See that guy over there? The one carrying the didgeridoo?"

Rhi gazed at the pony-tailed man with the long, thin didgeridoo slung across his shoulder. Long ... thin... She had seen that shape somewhere before...

"Mate!" Brody called, and the didge player stopped. "Love your didge. I don't suppose you were playing it late Friday night?"

"Sure was," said the player. "Out at the sweat lodge in the woods. Those dudes like night-time playing. You hear it or something?"

"We heard it all right," said Brody. "Saw it too, when you were heading back to your tent through the woods. Around four, wasn't it?"

The didgeridoo player nodded, smiling a grin peppered with gold teeth. "Night-time is the best time. Catch you around."

"There's your weird Friday-night animal, Rhi," Brody said as the musician made the peace sign at them both and carried on walking across the site with his didge across his shoulders.

Rhi felt fractionally better, although a little stupid. That was one mystery solved, at least. The other mystery however, remained as stubborn as ever.

"But what about Madame Felicity?" she pressed.

Brody squeezed her shoulders. "The organizers must have some record of her being here. She probably had to pay them to set up her stall."

Rhi's heart lifted. Brody really was on top form today. "Brilliant," she said in relief. "We'll find Kristina and Gerald, ask them to tell us where Madame Felicity went. You're right, they're bound to know."

Kristina and Gerald had a large red wagon on wheels, parked near the main stage, flying the symbol of the Oak Horse from its flagpole. Rhi and Brody climbed the wooden steps to the wagon's stable-like door, pushed aside the beaded curtain and peered inside.

"Hello?" Rhi called tentatively.

Kristina appeared, looking quizzically at them. Her

face cleared as she recognized Rhi and Brody, and she beckoned them inside.

"How can I help you, my dears?" she asked, as they perched a little awkwardly around a small wooden table with a central incense burner in the shape of a dragon.

"It's about one of your stallholders," Rhi began. "We're trying to find her, but we're not having any luck. We hoped you'd be able to help."

Kristina looked doubtful. "Gerald is the one who makes the bookings, dear – I'm not sure—"

"Taking my name in vain, Kris my love?" asked Gerald, clomping through the beaded curtains in an eye-wateringly bright kaftan and a strange hat. He took his hat off and hung it on a little peg by the wagon door.

"Gerald!" said Kristina, looking pleased. "Our two little minstrels are looking for a stallholder, I'm sure you'll be able to help."

"She's a fortune teller," Rhi said. "Madame Felicity?"

Kristina and Gerald seemed to freeze. There was a peculiar silence.

"Madame *Felicity*?" Kristina repeated, her eyes wide. "Are you sure that was her name, dear?"

"It was painted on the side of her wagon. Madame Felicity, truth-teller," Rhi explained. "She was tall, with white hair?"

"There's no one here by that name," said Gerald abruptly.

Kristina's eyes were darting around like a frightened animal. "I think you'd better go, my dears." She stood up from the little wooden table, wringing her hands anxiously. "I'm sorry we can't help you."

Rhi couldn't shake the strange atmosphere that had descended at the mention of Madame Felicity's name. She wondered if they'd offended this odd couple somehow. "Are you absolutely sure?" she tried one last time. "She was camping in the woods, not far from our tent. There was a brown and white horse..."

"We have to tell them the truth, Kris," said Gerald resignedly.

Kristina looked fearfully out of the window. "They don't need to know, Gerald. I'm sure this has all been a strange mistake—"

"Kris," said Gerald again, more firmly this time.

Rhi was starting to feel scared. She exchanged glances with Brody, who looked just as worried. What was the mystery about the fortune teller? Why were Kristina and Gerald looking so pale and shocked? Rhi wasn't sure she wanted to know. But there was no turning back now.

FIFTEEN

"Tea, Gerald," said Kristina, after a long pause. "I think we're all going to need it."

Gerald busied himself at the tiny kitchen as Kristina rifled through one of many little drawers and cubbyholes that lined the walls of the wagon. Rhi wondered what she was about to produce. Her imagination was firing in all directions now.

"Matches," explained Kristina, returning to the little table and lifting the lid on the dragon incense-burner. "And sage. We must protect ourselves before we go any further."

"A wise precaution," said Gerald as he filled an old brown teapot with some pungent leaves and boiling water.

Protect ourselves from what? Rhi thought anxiously. She found herself reaching for Brody's hand under the table and holding on tight for reassurance.

Kristina lit the sage leaves and wafted the smoke around the little room with what looked like a swan's feather. Rhi tried not to cough, but the smoke was pungent. She was relieved when Kristina opened the window and the smoke escaped outside. Gerald poured everyone a large mug of tea and sat down at the table beside his wife. The atmosphere was so serious, Rhi felt a little as if they were about to be told off by a teacher.

"Many years ago," Kristina began, "these woods formed part of a large, private estate belonging to a family named Fanshawe. Lord Fanshawe made his fortune in Queen Elizabeth's court, they say, from great adventuring on the high seas."

"Otherwise known as piracy," said Gerald in a more practical tone of voice. "Piracy was quite the thing in the sixteenth century."

Rhi took a sip of tea. It tasted a little too much like wood shavings for her taste, but the feel of the hot mug in her hands was as comforting as this conversation was strange.

"What does Lord Fanshawe have to do with Madame Felicity?" asked Brody.

Kristina and Gerald exchanged a significant glance which wasn't lost on Rhi.

"Lord Fanshawe built a great house with the money that he had made," Kristina went on. "The Fanshawe family prospered for the next three hundred years, building extensions on the house until it resembled a palace. Four hundred rooms, they say it had, in its heyday. Turrets, and a hothouse for fruit, a ballroom and music rooms, a garden that was the envy of all, a library containing thousands of valuable books.

"The tenth Lord Fanshawe was born into the splendour of his ancestors. Proud he was, and vain, and handsome. He took a tour of Europe, as was fashionable among the young privileged men of that time, buying art and sculpture – and finding himself a wife."

Rhi sipped her tea again, visualizing the great house, and the handsome lord, and his doubtless beautiful wife. It was a romantic story, but she had a nasty feeling there would be no fairy-tale ending.

"His wife Chiara was the daughter of an Italian

farmer," Kristina continued. "Lord Fanshawe's family weren't best pleased that he had married someone so far beneath him, and foreign to boot. He brought Lady Fanshawe home, and installed her at the great house, and gave her money to burn. But life in the country soon bored him, and so he left for London."

"Leaving his wife behind?" Brody asked, sounding surprised.

Gerald looked grim. "Indeed. And there, perhaps, lies the start of the rot."

Kristina shushed her husband. "When Lord Fanshawe eventually returned to his house and his wife some months later, he brought with him a party of young men and women – and a young and beautiful fortune teller that had been the talk of London."

Rhi felt a thrill of horror in the pit of her stomach. She couldn't stop listening now.

"There was a great party," Kristina continued. "Food and wine, grapes from the hothouse vines, music and dancing. The fortune teller was the star attraction. She read the fortunes of every person in the room. She foretold wealth and happiness for some, bankruptcy and death for others. She told the party that Lady Chiara Fanshawe was in love with another man."

"A gardener on the estate," Gerald interjected, keen to play a part in the story as it unfolded. "Lady Chiara had grown lonely in the big house, with servants who looked down on her, no friends, no husband. No one shared her language, even. She took solace by walking in the gardens."

Brody looked unconvinced. "That's hardly predicting the future," he said. "The fortune teller had probably heard some gossip."

Kristina held up her hand. "She also predicted that not only would Lord Fanshawe lose his wife, he would lose everything he loved before the next moonrise two days later. Lord Fanshawe scoffed at her, and threw her out of his house."

A gust of wind outside rattled the red wagon's little windows, making Rhi jump.

"Two days later there was a terrible fire," said Kristina quietly. "The likes of which had never been seen before. It razed that vast house to the ground, killing Lord Fanshawe's mother, aunt and house servants. Books, art, everything was lost."

"Everything?" Rhi whispered. The smoke from the burning sage still hung in the air. It didn't seem possible that the fortune teller's prediction had come true. From the way Kristina had been telling the story, the lord had unimaginable wealth, a vast house and estate...

Kristina gave a heavy sigh, and sipped her tea. "Everything," she confirmed. "Lord Fanshawe's ships – the foundation of the family fortunes – were all lost at sea in a terrible storm that same night. London's biggest bank had invested heavily in the ships, and it too lost every penny that it held – including all the gold that the family had amassed. Lady Chiara disappeared with her gardener. As for Lord Fanshawe, he vanished too." Kristina leaned inwards, fixing her eyes on Rhi's face. "He and the fortune teller were never seen again. Some say that they ran away together, but no one knows for sure. The fortune teller's name was—"

"Madame Felicity," Rhi whispered, and Kristina and Gerald both nodded silently.

It was a crazy story, but somehow Rhi couldn't help believing it. She felt questions crowding into her mind, but it was hard to know where to begin.

"The Fanshawe line was wiped out," Gerald

finished. "Lord Fanshawe never had any children, you see. The ruined house was left to moulder away. Anything valuable that remained was looted, the unburned stones and bricks taken away and used to build houses in the nearby village. The forest grew back. Within fifty years, it was as if the Fanshawes, with all their money and prestige and power, had never existed. Madame Felicity's prediction had been devastatingly accurate."

"So very sad," sighed Kristina over her tea.

"Wait, this was, what, a hundred and fifty years ago?" Brody asked, frowning. "Whatever her name was, the fortune teller would be dead by now."

There it was again. The significant glance between the older couple.

"Madame Felicity is said to haunt these woods," said Kristina. "She periodically reappears, to foretell the future. Did she foretell your future, my dear?"

Rhi's blood turned to ice. The caravan *had* seemed like something from another time, now that she came to think about it. The washing line, the horse, the kettle. Madame Felicity's clothes, long and old-fashioned… She nodded, answering the older woman's question.

Kristina looked grave. "I hope that her predictions were kind," she said.

"You don't believe all this, do you?" said Brody, jolting Rhi back to reality. "It's crazy! Ghosts don't exist, predictions aren't true!"

Rhi stared into Brody's concerned blue eyes. She felt as if she had been somewhere else, somewhere unreal for a while... She didn't know what to believe.

"Thank you for telling us the story," she said returning her gaze to Kristina and Gerald. "And for the tea."

"The Oak Horse protects where he can," said Gerald. "Thank you for joining us this weekend, my dears. Do come again, won't you?"

The expressions on Kristina and Gerald's faces were kind but serious as they showed Rhi and Brody out of the wagon.

"Seriously, Rhi," Brody said, as they made their way back to the ruins of their tent. "Those two are crazy. We knew that as soon as we arrived on Friday. Don't give them another thought, OK? Hippies are famously unorganized. I bet they don't even keep records of all the vendors and stallholders at this festival. This fortune teller you saw probably knew the local legend and used the name. It's a great story, the kind of thing that will always generate good business. There's always a simple explanation for these things."

Rhi let him take her hand. She could still smell the burning sage from the organizers' wagon and taste the pungent tea on her lips. "Don't tell the others," she said impulsively. "Promise!"

"Believe me," said Brody with feeling, "I'm not going to tell them a thing."

SIXTEEN

When Rhi and Brody got back to the campsite, Rhi's first thought was that someone had stolen their tent. *That's all we need!* she thought in dismay as she registered the empty space. *This really has been the worst—*

"I've packed it away," Ollie said, appearing from behind one of the trees. His normally cheerful face was locked into an annoyed expression. "No thanks to anyone else. It's wet and it will probably stink when Becca gets it home but that's hardly my problem, is it?"

"Thanks Ollie," said Rhi, trying to make her voice sound as normal as she could. "Where is, um, everyone else?"

"Who cares," Ollie grumbled. "I'll put the tent in the van. Pass me the keys, Brody."

Rhi looked around in vain for the others as Ollie marched towards the van with the tent. She had hoped that everyone would have patched things up by the time she and Brody got back to the campsite, but it looked as if she was wrong.

Hearing the sound of stifled sobbing, Rhi peered around one of the fatter tree trunks on the edge of the glade. Polly looked up at her with reddened eyes. "Ollie dumped me," she croaked. "I feel broken, Rhi!"

Rhi sank down on the ground beside her woebegone friend and put her arm around Polly's shoulders. "He's just hungry," she tried to console her. "You know what boys are like when they listen to their stomachs."

"I wish you hadn't kissed him," Polly whispered, knuckling her eyes with her fists. She looked a sorry sight in her rain-soaked dress and her rain-darkened hair plastered to her face. "I know it was all a mistake and everything, but I can't stop thinking about it and Ollie got mad at me."

Rhi helped Polly to her feet. "This place has driven us all a bit mad, I think," she said, trying not to think about the ghostly fortune teller and her silvery hair.

"But we'll be home soon, and then everything will go back to normal."

"Do you promise?" Polly looked at Rhi beseechingly. "Honestly?"

How am I supposed to promise something like that? Rhi thought hopelessly. But she nodded anyway, desperate for Polly to smile.

"Help me pack up the rest of our stuff, will you?" she coaxed. "The sooner we get back to Heartside Bay, the sooner we can fix all the things that have gone wrong."

They wearily gathered the remnants of their disastrous camping trip into bags: Becca's saucepans, someone's toothpaste tube half hidden in the soggy ashes of the fireplace. Brody took everything in silent relays to the van. Ollie stopped short on his return at the sight of Polly with Rhi, glared, and turned back to follow Brody to the van again. Polly seemed to hunch in on herself, silent and miserable.

Polly and Ollie can't *break up, Madame Felicity said Ollie was Polly's rock, past and future...* Rhi shook her head, reminding herself not to think about the fortune teller who had caused so many problems.

But it was impossible. The questions kept nagging in her mind. Where were Becca and Eve? Could they fix Lila and Josh? Rhi shook out a soggy rug and tried to fold it over her arm without getting too drenched.

Becca and Eve appeared as Brody packed the last bag into the van.

"Better late than never," he said a little drily.

Rhi threw him a warning glance but it was too late. Eve glared. "I don't need a lecture from you, Brody, thank you very much. I just want to get out of here."

"Make that two of us," Becca said. Judging from the freckled girl's set jaw and flinty expression, Becca hadn't made it up with Eve either.

The journey home is going to be one long party, Rhi thought to herself, and almost giggled at the horribleness of it all.

"Has anyone seen Josh or Lila?" she asked hopefully as Ollie, Eve, Polly and Becca stalked silently beside her towards where Brody was waiting in the van.

"Don't mention Josh Taylor's name to me," Lila snarled, appearing from nowhere with a fresh henna tattoo on her brown arm. "Guess what I caught him doing, barely five minutes after the biggest argument of our relationship? Drawing that flaming Oak Horse thing, like he didn't have a care in the world! Stupid idiot."

So that wasn't fixed either, Rhi thought with a sigh.

"This is all so stupid," Polly groaned.

"Don't call us stupid," Eve and Lila both snapped at once.

Rhi caught Becca's eye in silent sympathy. She wondered if they ought to round up Josh before Brody lost patience and started the engine, leaving Josh and his sketches behind. But as they piled into the back of the van – which smelled no better than it had on Friday – she glimpsed Josh's long-legged silhouette, hat perched on the back of his head, jogging towards the van with his sketch pad under his arm.

"Don't let him in, Brody," Lila snarled from her seat in the back. "He should be *walking* home."

Brody ignored her, opening the passenger door. "Hop in, mate," he advised. "It's a snake pit in the back. You'll be safer up front with me."

Rhi looked anxiously around at all her friends as Brody slammed the old van into first gear and they bumped away, out of the woods towards the road. Eve and Becca were looking determinedly out of opposite windows. Lila had lain full stretch on one of the seats and was clearly pretending to be asleep, to avoid making conversation. Polly was staring at her lap, the occasional tear plopping off the end of her nose, while Ollie had put his music on at full blast and was sitting as far away from Polly as he could. No one dared tell him to turn it down. The atmosphere was poisonous.

Rhi thought sadly of the name sprayed on the side of the van as they rumbled along a winding country lane towards the motorway. "Lovers and Losers" had never felt so apt. They might have started as lovers, but everyone was a loser now.

"Can't this tank go any faster?" Josh said after half an hour of deathly silence, with only the *boomboomboom* from Ollie's headphones to break the tension.

Brody frowned, studying the dashboard. "According to the speedo, it's going—"

The van shuddered, forcing Brody to break off his sentence and concentrate on keeping control of the wheel. Rhi didn't like the high-pitched, whining sound the engine was making. There was a sudden bang that made Lila scream as the engine failed completely and the van came to a grinding, groaning halt on the side of the road.

"What happened?" said Eve.

"We just got home," said Becca sarcastically. "What do you *think* happened, princess?"

Eve's grey eyes darkened to the colour of thunderclouds. "Don't you *dare* use that tone with me, Becca. I was only *asking*—"

Rhi had visions of dark smoke billowing out from underneath the van's pockmarked bonnet, the way it always seemed to happen in films. She scrambled out of her seat, pushing open the back doors. "Everyone out!" she ordered, visions of the whole vehicle going up in a vast fireball not far from her thoughts. "Stop arguing and get out, NOW!"

Everyone scrambled hurriedly out of the van. They had caught the clear sense of urgency in Rhi's voice. Josh and Brody were already out of the van and conferring in low voices on the side of the road.

"Oh, I'm fine, Josh, thanks for asking," Lila sniped, looking at her boyfriend sourly as he bent his head over his phone. "Don't worry about me, I just came this close to blowing up in the back of this stupid van—"

"Nothing's going to blow up, you idiot," said Josh, sounding unusually fierce. "I'm *trying* to call someone, OK? Or do you want to stay on the side of this road until nightfall?"

"No reception on my phone," Brody said. "Anything on yours, Ollie?"

Ollie shook his head. The others walked around the roadside, holding their phones high in the air, muttering and cursing.

Rhi looked up at the sloping sides of the valley reaching away from the road on either side of them. Valleys were famously bad for phone reception. Some sheep watched them with dull disinterest before returning to the hectic task of cropping the grass. A few birds wheeled away from them in the grey sky overhead. They were truly in the middle of nowhere.

"No one will ever find us!" Polly said, looking horrified. "We're in the middle of nowhere, no food, no water, nothing! What are we going to do?"

Becca rounded on Brody. "You took a weird shortcut," she accused, pointing at him. "We didn't come this way on Friday, what were you *thinking*?"

"Leave Brody alone, Becca," Eve shouted. "He was trying to get us home quicker, that's all. The sooner we get home, the sooner I can stop looking at your face, so that's just fine with me..."

Becca's face reddened. "I have had it with you, Eve, thinking you're better than everyone else—"

Rhi groaned and sank on to the verge as everyone descended into all-out war.

"I can't believe you called me an idiot, Josh, what the—"

"You are the most self-obsessed girl I have ever met, Lila—"

"It's Madame Felicity again, she's put a curse on us!" Polly wept, at Ollie, who was trying to speak over her, shouting: "Polly, you are completely *insane*..."

"Brody, we have to stop this!" Rhi begged her boyfriend, who was watching the chaos with a look of resignation on his face.

"They won't listen to me!" Brody protested.

Something burst inside Rhi. She ran towards her friends, her arms whirling above her head. "*Stop it!*"

she howled. "You're all behaving like lunatics! If you could *hear* yourselves... I would be laughing right now if this wasn't so utterly stupid. We are tearing ourselves apart, and why? Because of a *fortune teller*! A mad, white-haired old lady with a lump of glass and a horse! This is... You are... Just STOP!"

Her voice spiralled away in a screech that sent a covey of birds whirling up from the scrubby cover of the grass beside the road. Their snapping wings echoed around the valley like gunshots. Everyone stopped yelling.

"A dumb *horse*," Rhi repeated, glaring at her friends.

Everyone turned round at the sound of a strange snorting noise. Brody had his hands on his mouth, his white teeth gleaming between his fingers.

"What is so funny?" snapped Eve.

"The ... bit about ... about the horse," Brody managed in a sudden gust of laughter that echoed around the valley. "Blaming the *horse*..."

"Hey, *I* blame the horse," said Josh with a sudden flash of his old humour. "Four legs, mane, big teeth. What's to like?"

"The Oak Horse is strong in this one," Ollie

intoned, slipping his headphones off and dangling them sheepishly from his fingers.

Eve sat down very suddenly on the side of the road. "I like horses," she said, to no one in particular.

Brody's laughter was infectious. It started to spread, catching Josh and Ollie first, followed by Eve, and Lila, Becca and Polly. The sound bounced up and around the sides of the valley, and for a moment it felt as if the hillside sheep were laughing too. Rhi's mouth twitched.

"Lunatics," she repeated.

SEVENTEEN

Ollie held his arms out to Polly, who ran with a gasp of relief into his embrace. They stood on the spot, swaying for a moment.

"I'm sorry, Poll," Ollie said in a humble voice, stroking Polly's hennaed hair. "I do love you even though you are truly insane."

"Quit while you're ahead, Ollie," Brody advised, grinning.

Ollie looked alarmed. "I've said it all wrong again, haven't I?" he said in a worried voice. "I just... I don't want to lose you, Polly. You're the best thing in my life."

"That will do very nicely," Polly laughed through her tears. "I knew that fortune teller was right when she said you were my rock."

Ollie looked pleased. "She said that?"

Polly answered by reaching up on tiptoe to kiss her boyfriend on the lips. Ollie wrapped his arms around her and lifted her off the ground, and Rhi found herself averting her eyes and feeling shy, as if she was spying on something she had no right to see. *One down, two to go.*

Josh and Lila were still glaring at each other, and for a horrible moment Rhi thought they were going to start arguing again. Then a faint smile glimmered on Josh's face.

"Idiot," he said to Lila. He reached out to twist a single lock of Lila's dark hair around his fingers and tug her towards him.

Lila caught his hand and held it. "Horse-hater," she replied. She tossed her hair in the manner of a horse flicking its mane out of its eyes, and giggled.

She and Josh fell into each other's arms and kissed each other so passionately that Rhi half expected the grass to burst into flames around their feet.

"There's other people here, you know," Ollie observed with Polly nestled up against his shirt. Josh and Lila didn't appear to hear him.

"I'm sorry about the 'girls' thing, Becs." Eve looked more awkward than Rhi had ever seen her. "There's only one girl. You."

"That's more like it," said Becca with a nod.

And then they were kissing too, their eyes closed and their arms wrapped tightly around each other with Becca's fingers twining lovingly through Eve's hair.

Rhi felt relief coursing through her. Everything was back to normal. This whole weekend had been a strange blip in their lives, never to be repeated. She didn't want any of this to change, ever again.

Brody nudged her. "Fancy a walk?" he asked. "I don't know about you, but I don't think these guys will notice our absence."

Rhi giggled. Her friends were so wrapped up in their partners again, it was as if she and Brody were invisible. She waited by the side of the road as Brody fetched his guitar from the van, and slung the strap around his shoulder.

"Don't you ever stop singing?" she teased.

"Depends on my mood," he replied.

His eyes searched hers. Rhi felt uneasy. The kiss

she'd shared with Ollie was looming between them again. "So," she said, keen to break the silence. "Where shall we go?"

"Somewhere we can get phone reception so we can call for a breakdown truck," Brody replied, breaking eye contact for a moment as he pulled out his phone to check the signal. "How about up there?" He nodded towards the crest of the valley.

There was a stile a little further along the road, and a path that snaked up the hill along the side of a scruffy-looking hedge. Leaving the reunited couples to their kisses and apologies, Rhi and Brody walked together, puffing a little on the steep incline, dodging the sheep dung and the uneven crumbling ground where the local rabbits had made their warrens.

Around halfway up, Rhi paused to admire the view, but Brody kept walking, head down and his brow furrowed, his blond hair whipping around his head in the wind and his guitar bouncing on his back. She tore her eyes away with a sigh and followed him. He showed no sign of waiting for her.

"Brody, what's the hurry?" she called, feeling a flutter of annoyance. "Wait for me!"

The ground up here was flatter, the sheep-nibbled hilltop crowned with a scattering of boulders. Brody was sitting on the largest rock, his legs swinging, his fingers idly plucking at his guitar as Rhi panted towards him.

The view made Rhi catch her breath for real. They could see most of the coastline, even the distant headland around which she knew Heartside Bay and normal life would be waiting. *School life*, she realized. Term started tomorrow. Brody had left school already, and wouldn't be with her so much for a while. That was a strange thought.

Rhi moved her gaze away from the coast, focusing inland instead, enjoying the sight of rolling hills and woodland in a vast green and brown speckled blanket. The van was little more than a grey speck on the winding steel ribbon of road far below them; the others flecks of coloured dust on the verge.

"Thanks for waiting," Rhi joked as she scrambled up to join him.

Brody strummed a chord and didn't answer. Feeling uneasy all over again, Rhi sat beside him. They stayed still for a while, staring out to sea.

"The world is so much bigger than we realize," Brody said. "Isn't it?"

Rhi frowned. "That's very philosophical," she said, trying to jolly Brody out of the odd mood that had descended.

Brody smiled slightly. "That's me. Deep."

He bent his head over his strings, playing an absent-minded riff. Rhi shot her boyfriend several troubled glances. What was this undercurrent she was sensing?

You know what it is, whispered the voice in her head, but she didn't want to listen.

"The music in you and the music in me," Brody sang, almost to himself. "They tie us together while making us free, they tie us together while making us free…"

Rhi found herself stiffening. Brody stopped mid-chord and glanced at her.

"You really don't like that song, do you? Why not?"

"Because it makes out that music is the only thing we have," said Rhi. She felt upset even saying the thought out loud.

"The song is the magic, the tune is the spell," Brody sang, watching her. "And we are magicians to weave them so well, and we are magicians to weave them so well... What did Madame Felicity say about us, exactly?"

Rhi felt alarmed at the sudden pause in the song, the change of conversational direction. "She was just a mad old lady with a horse," she fudged. "What she said is irrelevant."

"Rhi, I'd like to know," Brody said patiently. He gestured at the air between them. "Lila mentioned something about us not being together."

Rhi caught Brody's hand. She didn't want to remember the fortune teller's violet eyes or her sad predictions. "What would a fortune teller know about us? About the way we feel about each other?"

"What did she say, Rhi?" he repeated.

Rhi gulped. "She said ... she said our music will endure. Our partnership..." *Do not mistake what you have, my dear...* Unable to voice her fears, she took Brody's face between her palms instead and gazed into his blue eyes, willing him to believe that everything was fine, that they were meant to be together... "I love you," she said a little desperately, "you're the best thing that's ever happened to me, you've shown me the kind of artist that I can be!" And she moved to kiss him.

As he kissed her back, Rhi had a brief flash memory of how she had felt when Max – wicked, cheating Max – had kissed her. There had been real passion there. He had been no good for her, but the attraction had been undeniable. With Brody ... dearest, loveliest Brody ... the spark wasn't there. He treated her so wonderfully, he was her best friend, their shared passion for music held the key... *Do not confuse the muse with love.*

Brody took her hands and lowered them again. "You can't kiss this better, Rhi," he said.

Rhi felt a rush of miserable anger. "We can't let a fortune teller ruin what we have!"

Brody's eyes widened, and she knew at once that she'd said too much. She had confirmed his fears. Madame Felicity had spelled their doom.

"Brody, no..." she whispered as he took off his guitar and laid it on the rock beside them and looked into her eyes. "Don't do this. Don't..."

She knew as surely as if he'd said the words already.

He was going to break up with her.

EIGHTEEN

"Please don't," said Rhi, taking Brody's hands. "Don't break us up, Brody, please..."

There were tears in Brody's eyes as well. "Shh, Rhi, don't cry, you're setting me off. I'm not breaking us up – I'm just... It's time to break up the part of us that isn't meant to be."

This couldn't be happening... "Brody—"

Brody rubbed his eyes. "I love you, Rhi. I can't be without you, you complete me. When we make music, it's perfect. We are destined always be together, OK? Making music together. Always. Just..."

"Not like this," Rhi whispered, finishing the sentence for him.

He touched her cheek with the back of his hand.

"This isn't true love," he said, smiling through his tears. "Is it?"

Rhi sniffed. "Are you saying you don't fancy me any more?" she joked feebly.

He looked at her with serious eyes. "Rhi, you are the most beautiful girl I've never known. Inside and out. I wish we could be together *and* make music together, but we can't. The music is too special to risk. And I know you agree with me, because I know you so well, Rhi Wills."

Rhi covered her face with her hands and sobbed. Brody stroked her back, curling his fingers through her hair and whispering soothing words. She felt devastated, but she knew Brody was right. In a funny way, the more she cried, the more clear-headed she became. Now that the thing she had been dreading had finally happened, she could at last see the way ahead.

We broke up, she thought, testing the feeling in her head. *But we're going to be OK.*

She wiped her eyes with trembling hands and then wrapped her arms around Brody. He hugged her, and kissed her cheek.

"I do love you," he said against her hair. "I'll always love you."

"You're wonderful, you know," said Rhi, feeling both sad and shy as they broke apart again. "The right girl for you is out there, I'm sure she is. And when you find her, I hope she realizes how lucky she is."

"And you are going to have guys queuing round the block for you," he said, half-smiling. "To tell the truth, they already do."

Rhi struck him lightly on the shoulder, flushing. "Hardly!" she protested, laughing and crying at the same time.

"I'm completely serious. They line up for you after each gig. Which is why I always make sure that I have my arm around you whenever we come off the stage. In case they get ideas."

Rhi laughed again in disbelief. Brody laughed back, acknowledging his underhand methods. "I promise I'll stop doing that now," he said.

Rhi tried to imagine who her next boyfriend might be, if perhaps he had heard one of her gigs already and stood in that line Brody had told her about. Her stomach stirred with anticipation. It was fun, the whole looking-for-the-next-guy-to-fancy thing. She was half looking forward to it already, and half not.

"You OK?" Brody asked.

Rhi knew the ache in her heart would improve with time. She nodded. "You?"

"Mustn't grumble."

It was such an old-mannish thing to say that Rhi had to laugh. "Will you sing something with me?" she asked. It seemed the right way to round off what they'd had together, to start the next phase with a song.

Brody took up the guitar and brushed his fingers lightly over the strings. They shivered sweetly. "Any requests?"

"'Being Me'," said Rhi, after thinking about it for a while. "The lyrics feel appropriate. You make me, me," she said simply.

"I'm glad," came his reply.

Their voices came together, arcing through the air, spinning out towards the woods and the hills and the glittering sea in the distance, and they sounded good – better, even, than Rhi had ever imagined. The musical connection was back, sharp and clear and stronger than ever. How could she have doubted it? How could she have risked losing this?

"Being me, is harder than I want it to be," they sang, Rhi's head resting on Brody's shoulder. "Being me, is riding out the waves in the sea, being me is harder than a diamond in the ground, but being you doesn't work, I've found..."

The song was about being true to who you were, driving through life with yourself at the wheel and nobody else, and Rhi felt as free as the birds wheeling overhead as she sang, the sound of Brody's guitar wrapping itself around their voices in a shining golden thread...

"It's all about yourself, ain't nobody else, there's only one of you before they broke the mould," they sang, Brody taking the harmony and Rhi the tune. "Don't be afraid to fail the grade, you gotta cry before you fly, it's the golden reason why ... you are you and I am me... And that's the truth of it, you see... Being me..."

Rhi shifted so that she could look right into Brody's crystal blue eyes and he could look right back at her and see her for who she was. He would never hurt her, he would never leave her. The selfish business of love seemed irrelevant, compared to that.

"That's the truth of all we see," they sang in unison – loath to break the spell but knowing the song was nearing its natural end – "being me."

The wind lifted the final chords and whipped them away over Rhi and Brody's heads, echoing them weirdly among the rocks before taking them up into the clouds and the air. Rhi felt a sort of peace settling on her, and knew Brody was feeling it too.

"Weird weekend, huh?" he said.

"So weird," Rhi sighed.

Her phone bleeped, breaking the moment.

"And reality intrudes," Brody kissed Rhi on the forehead, a sweet and final kiss, as Rhi took out her phone and stared at the message.

Truck's fine! Don't know what happened, Josh turned engine and everything just worked. And I have signal suddenly too! CRAZZYY TIMES!!! Lxxxx

160

"That's impossible," said Brody, staring at the screen over Rhi's shoulder.

Magic, Rhi thought absently. "I guess the truck was just tired," she said, wiping her cheeks, getting off the rock and brushing herself down.

"The engine was dead," Brody protested. He started following her towards the path again, and down the hillside. "Kaput. How can it just *work*? No mechanics, no tools, no breakdown truck, nothing?"

"Stop asking questions!" Rhi called back at him. She needed to concentrate on where she put her feet as they slipped and slid down the steep hill towards the six dots that comprised their friends. "Just be grateful there won't be a breakdown bill!"

She could see their friends waving their arms way, way below them. A little plume of exhaust smoke was issuing from the back of the van and spiralling its way up the valley. The smoke twisted around itself, forming for an instant what looked to Rhi like a figure in a long dress, glowing white hair trailing down her back.

The smoke broke apart again lazily, almost before Rhi had caught and pinned the thought in her mind. She could hear the engine now, chugging patiently below them. She hopped over a tuft of grass, and almost fell over with shock at the brown streak that hurtled away across the hillside from beneath her feet. A hare, to judge from the black tips on the ends of its over-large ears. It sped from sight, its white tail flashing.

More magic, Rhi thought, wondering. *It seems that you were right after all, Madame Felicity. Whoever you were.*

NINETEEN

Of all the days for her phone not to work… Rhi rammed her toast between her teeth and scooped up her bag, her nerves jangling. Her uniform felt tight, as if she had grown over the summer. The waistband was definitely pinching and the skirt was way shorter than it had been back in July. Rhi tugged it irritably, showering toast crumbs on her black-and-red blazer.

"Are you still here, Rhi?" said her mother, putting her head disapprovingly out of the study door. "You're normally halfway to school by now."

Rhi swallowed the over-large piece of toast, almost choking in the process. "I know, don't nag me," she said hopelessly. "My alarm didn't go off…"

Her mother's eyes narrowed. Dr Wills was a stickler

for punctuality. "Your first day back and already late? Not good enough, Rhi," she said. "I hope you're going to take this year more seriously than last. You have—"

"GCSEs at the end of the year, I know, Mum," said Rhi, doing her best not to roll her eyes. "This was just a blip, OK? We got back late last night – totally out of our control, the van broke down – so I didn't get much sleep, but honestly, everything will be fine. I'll make registration, I promise. I'll just be more out of breath than normal."

"And more covered in toast!" her mother shouted after her with an unusual flash of humour as Rhi rushed for the door, slamming it hard behind her, and set off as briskly as she could without giving herself indigestion.

As she walked, she tried not to think about the state her hair was in. She had meant to have a long shower this morning, conditioning the terrible tangle on her head, but she'd barely had time to wash her face. *Stupid phone...* she thought with irritation. She could still feel toast crumbs around her mouth, but she licked her lips as best she could and made a mental note to double-check her reflection in the bathroom when she made it into school.

Kids in uniform swarmed up the wide white steps in front of her, pushing through the double doors, talking and laughing and shouting. New kids in blazers way too big for them stood in nervous huddles at the foot of the steps, trying to work out when to take the plunge into the flowing black and red river. Rhi remembered her first day at Heartside High with a flash of nostalgia. She could hardly believe she was in year eleven already. Where had the time gone? The summer had flashed past like lightning, and here she was again, back on the old treadmill.

Her phone buzzed. Pulling her bag from her shoulder, Rhi read the text.

RU OK? Bx

Brody's texts were always brief, but this one was even more brief than normal. She keyed in a simple smiley face and sent it back, thoughtfully. How did she feel about Brody today?

They'd all got back so late from the Oak Horse Festival last night, and she'd been so tired after two nights of badly broken sleep and a great deal of emotion, that the moment her head had touched her blissfully soft pillow she had crashed into a dreamless sleep and not given Brody or their break-up a single thought. Now she prodded her heart cautiously. It felt a little bruised, but that was the most that she could find to say about it.

Was it possible to get over someone so quickly?

Their song on the hilltop had helped, she decided. They'd broken up gently and lovingly, and that had helped too. Would they be able to maintain their musical connection now that their relationship was over? The signs were good. Rhi took heart from that. She felt nervous thinking about the next time she'd see him, of course she did. She was only human. She didn't know what she would say. But for now, at least—

Her face made contact with the front of a blazer as she cannoned straight into someone standing still on the steps.

"OW!" Rhi pulled back, rubbing her nose, her eyes watering like mad, and stared at the person she'd struck. *Please don't get a nosebleed*, she thought randomly. *Right now a nosebleed would be really bad.*

Because she found herself looking at the handsomest face she'd ever seen.

The boy had close-cropped dark hair and skin that was either naturally olive or the product of an expensive holiday abroad. His eyes were jet black, his nose perfectly straight. In the chaos of first impressions, Rhi couldn't decide if his sculpted mouth with its set of perfect white teeth was smiling at her, or snarling.

"I . . . sorry, I wasn't looking where I was going. . ." Rhi said, staring at him a little helplessly. Why hadn't she woken up earlier this morning, managed a shower? Her hair probably looked like a hedge right now. And not a touch of make-up! She wanted to groan at the unfairness of the situation. "People don't normally stop on these steps."

"Everyone does seem to be in a rush, don't they?" he said. He brushed at his jacket with one hand, as if Rhi had smudged it in some way. "I can't imagine why. It's only school."

He was new, Rhi realized. She made a few frantic calculations, trying to guess his age, wondering if he would be joining her year. "I'm Rhi," she said, and stuck out her hand politely.

He ignored it. "I know who you are," he said, sounding a little bored. "You're the local talent, aren't you? You and your boyfriend perform at that scruffy little café near the waterfront."

Rhi felt a rush of annoyance. "My dad runs the Heartbeat Café," she said stiffly, withdrawing her hand. "It's a great place. Everyone hangs out there." Did she have toast crumbs all around her mouth? She had a horrible feeling there was a smear of butter on her chin too.

"Oh. Sorry," said the boy, not looking in the least bit apologetic. To make things worse, he laughed, giving Rhi another flash of his perfect teeth.

"And Brody's not my boyfriend." Rhi wasn't sure why she bothered adding this piece of information. *I'm just testing it out,* she thought to herself. *Seeing how it sounds out loud. I am absolutely NOT giving this guy any signals whatsoever that I am single.*

She wondered distractedly if he had a girlfriend, and immediately hated herself for wondering. Boys like this probably had a different girlfriend for every day of the week.

He was looking away from her already, assessing

the crowds as they flowed around the two of them like a river flowing past two rocks. Checking for someone more interesting to talk to, Rhi realized irritably. She resolutely ignored her disappointment.

"Whatever," he said, squinting at the faces as they passed. "I'm Tristan de Vere. Just moved here. Mum's been hired to sort out your shopping centre. It's a mess, apparently. The last guy turned out to be a fraudster, can you believe it?"

The irritation Rhi was feeling crystallized into pure dislike as he laughed. Tristan de Vere – could that name be any snootier if it tried? It matched him perfectly.

The fraudster you're laughing about happens to be the father of one of my best friends, she thought, feeling overwhelmed with rage. Who did he think he was, mouthing off about her town and her friends in this way? It was unbelievable. Everything about Tristan de Vere – the way he stood there sneering at the crowd, squinting his black eyes and wrinkling up his perfect nose in distaste – screamed arrogance. Rhi wasn't the confrontational type, but even she had her limits.

She opened her mouth, fully prepared to give him a piece of her mind about his attitude and sheer rudeness.

She didn't care what might come out. All she cared about was wiping the sneer off his extraordinarily handsome face.

"Sorry," Tristan said, suddenly switching his gaze back to her. "You probably think I'm really rude. I don't mean to mouth off about stuff that probably matters to you. When you've lived in Paris, New York and London, it's hard to take a little place like this seriously."

Rhi gaped at him. Not only had he taken the wind out of her sails with his sudden apology, he'd managed to turn the apology into yet another insult! As she grappled with something to come back at him with, he gave a sigh of resignation.

"Getting used to this crappy little seaside town is going to take some time, but I guess I'll manage it. Not like I have much choice in the matter. See you around."

"I... You..."

But Tristan had gone, loping away up the remaining steps to the glass doors at the top. Rhi stared at his broad back as it disappeared inside the building, swallowed up in the tide.

"Arrgh!" she screamed in frustration, startling a

pair of very small Year Eights as they scurried past her. Tristan de Vere was possibly the most infuriating boy she had ever met.

And just maybe, said a very small voice in her head, *the hottest.*

"Shut up," Rhi muttered at herself. "You are *so* not going there."

TWENTY

Rhi roused herself after a few more seconds of standing stupidly on the steps. Her veins still fizzed with rage. She had to get to class. She was already late, for goodness' sake.

She ploughed through the milling crowds in the reception area, dashing into the first girls' bathroom she could find. She stared at herself in dismay. The bathroom mirror proved that things were even worse than she had thought. Not only was her hair a perfect ball of frizz, there was sleepy dust in the corners of her eyes, toast all over her blazer and her pillow had left a crumpled imprint on one cheek. She looked like a wild-eyed lunatic.

Forget him, she ordered herself. *What are you interested in a snob like that for anyway?*

Brushing away the toast crumbs, washing her face, wetting her hair and applying a quick dash of lipgloss fixed the worst of the problems, although the crease mark in her cheek remained stubbornly where it was. Rhi left the bathroom and set off in determination towards where she hoped her new classroom might be. She'd been in such a rush that morning that she'd had no time to study the information they'd all been handed at the end of the previous term. She tried to keep familiar faces within her sights, and hoped they would take her in roughly the right direction.

As she turned down the year eleven corridor, she glimpsed Tristan de Vere's tall dark head almost at once, making its way easily through the throng. Her heart gave a treacherous leap. He was in her year after all.

Like that matters, she thought fiercely. *I wish he was year ten. I wish he wasn't here at all.*

Still, she found her eyes glued to the back of his head as they approached the classrooms. There were five tutor groups. There was a twenty per cent chance that Tristan would be in hers.

"Gotcha!"

Rhi had been concentrating so hard on not losing

sight of Tristan, that the sudden appearance of her friends from a side corridor startled the life out of her. They were all there – Eve, Josh, Lila, Polly and Ollie – all grinning, all asking her questions. It felt as if they hadn't seen each other for weeks.

"Rhi, I've been texting you all morning," said Lila, linking arms with Rhi as they reached the new year eleven lockers. "I've been so worried about you."

Rhi's brain felt fuzzy. "Worried about what?"

"You and *Brody* of course!" said Polly anxiously. "Are you feeling awful? You didn't sleep well, did you? I can tell from the pillow crease on your face."

"Being dumped is the *worst* thing," said Lila with feeling.

"Like you'd know anything about it, Lila. Josh and you dumped each other for about half an hour yesterday," said Eve. "For Rhi, this is the real deal."

"I wasn't dumped," Rhi protested as Eve gave her a hug. "I'm fine, honestly."

"She's not well," Ollie remarked to Josh as Eve, Lila and Polly all tutted at Rhi in disbelief. "Girls never act normal when relationships end. She'll have a meltdown by break time, you watch."

174

"I am here, you know," Rhi said as Ollie and Josh both snorted with laughter. "And I don't plan on having any meltdowns any time soon, OK?"

"That's the thing about meltdowns," Eve said sagely. "They catch you when you least expect them."

"We'll be here for you, whatever," Polly added.

Rhi looked at her friends with mingled affection and annoyance. She loved them all, but they drove her nuts.

She suddenly became aware that Tristan was watching their group, leaning against the lockers with a look of sardonic amusement on his face. Her skin prickled self-consciously as he walked towards them with his hands rammed in his pockets.

"Hey," said Tristan, looking at her with his black eyes. "What was your name again?"

Great, Rhi thought irrationally. *I'm even more unmemorable than I thought.*

Ollie and Josh both frowned at the newcomer. Polly gaped; Eve folded her arms in a show of nonchalance that Rhi knew at once betrayed acute interest. Lila's baby-blue eyes widened.

"Who are *you*?" she breathed, looking Tristan up and down very slowly. "Rhi, who is this person?"

175

The most horrible boy in the world, Rhi wanted to shout. "The new boy," she said through gritted teeth.

"My, how exciting," Eve drawled, assessing Tristan with her sharp grey eyes. "Hello, new boy. Does he have a name, Rhi?"

"Tristan de Vere." The smile Tristan bestowed on Eve was dazzling.

You're wasting your energies there, Rhi thought, as a flash of amusement pierced her simmering sense of resentment.

"Aren't you going to introduce me to your little friends, Rhi, or am I going to have to do it myself?" Tristan inquired.

Ollie took a step towards Tristan. They were almost the same height. "There's no one 'little' here, mate," he said, in a voice bristling with hostility.

Polly laid her hand on Ollie's arm. "Don't mind Ollie, he's never very good in the mornings," she said, smiling shyly at Tristan. "Welcome to Heartside Bay."

"You are *extremely* welcome," said Lila coquettishly. "I can't tell you how bored I am of looking at all the same old faces, and I've only been here two terms. You are going to make a *very* pleasant change."

"You look like you know where to find a good party," said Tristan, grinning at Lila. "Give me your number?"

"My, you're a fast worker," Lila purred.

"I'd prefer it if you didn't chat up my girlfriend, mate," said Josh, looking sourer than ever.

"Claimed are you? Shame," said Tristan. His gaze flitted towards Eve.

"She's claimed too," said Polly with a giggle.

It was very unlike Polly to giggle around boys, Rhi thought. Tristan had some kind of magic touch.

"And by someone more different from you than you could possibly imagine," Eve added. Her grey eyes sparkled. "But don't let that stop you trying."

"Who *is* this clown, Rhi?" Ollie demanded.

"Eve, Polly, Lila, Josh and Ollie," Rhi reeled off reluctantly. "Meet Tristan. We bumped into each other outside just now."

"Lucky you," said Eve, acerbically.

All three girls appeared spellbound by the newcomer. Ollie and Josh, not so much. Rhi started to get a sinking feeling about Tristan de Vere.

The bell rang harshly in the corridor.

"You're making us late already, Tristan," said Lila, linking arms with the dark-haired boy. "You are going to be a bad influence, I can tell."

"I'll try my best," Tristan replied, smirking.

Josh and Ollie shoved past Tristan and into the classroom, jostling him against the doorframe.

"Don't be an oaf, Ollie," hissed Polly as Lila exclaimed and apologized and dusted off Tristan's broad shoulders a little more lingeringly than necessary. "What's Tristan going to think?"

"I don't give a stuff what he thinks about anything," Ollie shot back, before stalking off to join an equally sulky-looking Josh at the back of the classroom.

Rhi had a very good idea what Tristan was going to think. She followed the others into the classroom, biting her lip to see how her three friends were all giggling around the newcomer, settling him in at his desk. Tristan was clearly loving the attention.

With a sudden nasty lurch, Rhi pictured a crystal ball on a velvet-covered table, the smell of wood smoke in the air and the sound of a horse munching its way through a tattered old nosebag. She sat down slowly at her desk, her mind spinning in a hundred different directions, none of them as good. The stranger. The boy in the heart of the crystal ball.

Resting her head on her desk, Rhi closed her eyes, doing her best to block out the sound of Polly's giggles and Lila's flirtatious tone of voice. Madame Felicity had been right so far. She had a horrible feeling she was right about Tristan de Vere as well.

Beware the stranger in your midst. He brings dark discord.

It looked like the dark discord had already begun.

LOOK OUT FOR MORE

HEARTSIDE BAY

Life, love and everything in between

HEARTSIDE BAY

The
New Girl

CATHY COLE

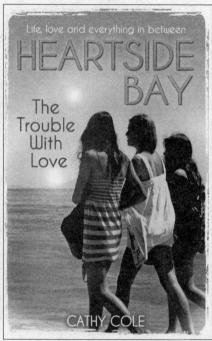

Life, love and everything in between

HEARTSIDE BAY

The
Trouble
With
Love

CATHY COLE

Life, love and everything in between

HEARTSIDE BAY

More
Than a
Love
Song

CATHY COLE

Life, love and everything in between

HEARTSIDE BAY

A
Date
With
Fate

CATHY COLE

Life, love and everything in between

HEARTSIDE BAY

Never
a Perfect
Moment

CATHY COLE

Life, love and everything in between

HEARTSIDE BAY

Kiss at
Midnight

CATHY COLE

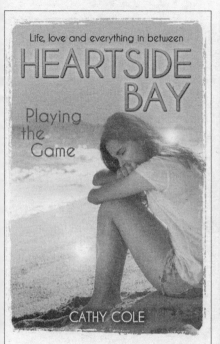

Life, love and everything in between

HEARTSIDE BAY

Playing
the
Game

CATHY COLE

Life, love and everything in between

HEARTSIDE BAY

Flirting
With
Danger

CATHY COLE